*To the liars and killers who make me a better man*

# CRISIS BOY

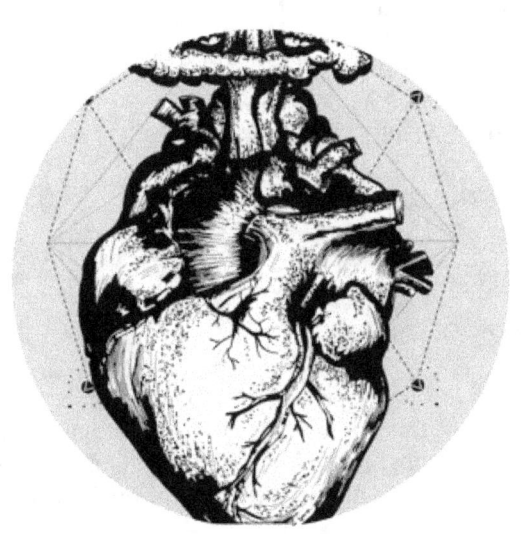

# GARRETT COOK

deadite press

# deadite press

DEADITE PRESS
P.O. BOX 10065
PORTLAND, OR 97296
www.DEADITEPRESS.com

AN ERASERHEAD PRESS COMPANY
www.ERASERHEADPRESS.com

ISBN: 978-1-62105-268-5

*Crisis Boy* copyright © 2018 by Garrett Cook

Cover design by Deadite Press

Printed in the USA.

# THE MOTHERFUCKING DEVIL

John was all of ten years old when he came face to thousand yard face with the motherfucking devil. The motherfucking devil had a briefcase in an elementary school and had come to do terrible work. John would meet the devil many times over but on this day, the motherfucking devil went by the name Adam Lanza. At ten he was too old to be in the monster's sights, but he coughed from around the corner and that cough let the motherfucking devil know that he'd been made.

That's when they locked eyes, John and the Devil. That's when he first stared past miles of no damn good to find fear, confusion and despair, to find the notion that none of all this was worth shit and that he was doing everyone a favor and that he was about to do John a favor. He had shot his way in unceremoniously and John would be no more of an obstruction than that glass door had been.

A loud report, a buzzing, a ringing. Seven burning beestings slammed into John's chest, his gut and out his back. John hit the floor, spraying out more than he knew he even had as he went down hard. He closed his eyes, he held his breath, excruciating since one bullet had punctured his lung. He waited and listened, then let his eye open a crack and saw Lanza keep walking, saw a tiny figure's pink coat splatter red, black brown with splinters of bone.

The Devil had kept going, walking into a classroom and unloading on the first graders. And then, when the Devil was finished, he had chosen another classroom and John could still hear the screaming, the sound of students herded into the bathroom by brave teachers that would surely be punished for taking the hunter's quarry from him. He waited, he bled and he listened and he hoped idly that he would never again make the acquaintance of the motherfucking Devil.

There was one last merciful gunshot, a single time the Devil had chosen right. John had never laid still for so long in his life and soon, it would be over, like the life of the unstoppable monster who had filled him with those bullets. He should have felt a sense of relief as he was led out on the gurney but instead of that he'd come away with the knowledge that monsters walk among us.

# AGAIN, THE MOTHERFUCKING DEVIL

John was at the starting line and he was waiting. He was wondering what it was like to wait for something nice. There was Christmas. He knew what it was like to wait for Christmas and Christmas was nice enough but it was not so nice that it was as nice as what was happening was terrible. They had tried to tell him that it was nice that he was waiting for history. John was not sure he really liked making history. The last time he had, he'd been perforated with bulletholes. This time it was likely to be worse.

He looked at his phone to see if he'd have time to grab an iced coffee from the Dunkin Donuts across the street. It was possible that he might have had time to grab an iced coffee from the Dunkin Donuts across the street. He'd had one in the morning but he still felt like having another. Or a lemonade Coolatta. A lemonade Coolatta might be nice. Or an Italian ice. Maybe he could find a slice of pizza.

He texted his mom.

"Would I have time to grab a slice of pizza?"

"Do not grab a slice of pizza."

"How about an iced coffee?"

"Do not grab an iced coffee."

"I'm kinda thirsty."

"You don't have time. Stay where you are."

He sighed. He really wanted a slice now. At least not getting a slice wasn't going to be the worst thing that happened to him today. And it certainly wouldn't have been the worst thing to happen to the people around him. So he switched over to Tetris and waited. He was one of many people staring down at their phone and standing around but he was one of the only ones to know that what they were waiting for was not the marathon.

The motherfucking devil wore another skin today as he was wont to do. He had been told to make this less about who these people are and to be less afraid of them. They weren't going to hurt him, not really. But they were certainly going to hurt the mothers holding up their kids, they were certainly going to hurt the volunteers with water bottles and shirts. They were certainly going to hurt the strong, lithe and determined athletes who had been working for this day. He had been told not to think of those who made these things happen as the motherfucking devil but it was very hard not to and he wouldn't be alone in these sentiments.

The devil today was calling himself Tsarnaev, one of two brothers. He wasn't going to be eye to eye with him like he was with Lanza. This was bigger, less personal. This wasn't about murder, it was about fear. He tried to imagine what sort of person would go this far just to make people afraid and once again, his mind raced to the devil. His stomach churned and he no longer wanted the pizza.

And then the windows blew out and in. And then the glass began to fly. And then the dust began to fly. And then people gathered around the starting line began to fly, launched into the air by cataclysmic loudness, burning wind and impact. He felt his eardrums cave in, felt the heat, felt the shockwave, felt himself carried aloft before landing hard. The limbs were beginning to fly, the cloud of blood and punishment, bone shrapnel, a rain of dust and skin and innards. Flesh was bubbling together, human meat superheating and smelling terribly crispy. Chaos and crying and shuffling and barking police dogs and screams and screams and screams and screams and screams and screams and an eternity before sirens and ambulances, short though that eternity might have been.

He lay on the ground again surrounded by the mangled, legs cut off at the knees, arms blown out of sockets, heads bent into puppet angles, lolling melted tongues glomping out the side of their dead faces, blood and asphalt, crisp and splinter and bone and indistinct once human ooze. He lay on the ground surrounded by figures laid out like the bomb was a petulant child and the marathon its toybox. He still sort of wanted an iced coffee. It was suddenly so damned hot.

As Rudy Kazanian sat at home and watched the explosion on the news, he could swear he'd seen one of the kids being dragged into an ambulance before. As the kid was John, Rudy Kazanian was in fact correct.

# THE MOTHERFUCKING
# DEVIL STRIKES ONCE MORE

John, being a boy, had been instructed not to go into the ladies' room. Because of this, John missed the worst parts of one of the worst massacres in American history. He could hear the screams from in there and was old enough to know what they meant. He knew why they were screaming "no, please, you can't!"

He had been warned that boys were headed for the girls' room. He had thought that this was the Colonel being crazy. Why would men go into the girls' room? Well, the answer was now clear, piercing and cruel. The Colonel wasn't always being crazy. There were fate worse than death screams. These were not unlike the "holy shit, where's my fucking leg?" screams. He had lost his fucking leg before and the current screams made that look quite favorable to whatever was going on in there.

"Allahu Akbar!" came the great war whoop.

Fuck. There were boys in the girls' room and they were Muslims. Like the guy who'd set off the bomb and the guys who had shot up the concert. Fuck. Muslims could disguise themselves as girls and make their way into the girls' room. There were screams but there were no gun shots or bombs. Surely some brave citizen would pull out his gun and make his way into the bathroom and shoot these Muslim men who had disguised themselves as women before they could murder anyone else in the ladies' room.

The manager of the Old Country Buffet looked around the room. It seemed he was thinking the same thing as John. For fuck's sake, it was an Old Country Buffet. Somebody had to be packing but there were no guns pulled. There were no heroes dashing into the ladies' room to kill these heretical female impersonators.

"Fuck," said the manager with a sigh, "this is what happens when we let men into the ladies' room."

"Enough, heretics!" screamed a vicious Muslim lady impersonator as it emerged from the bathroom, brandishing a scimitar.

Several diners tried to make their way to the entrance but found that there was already a blockade of men in dresses wielding swords and praising Allah. Since none were carrying guns, none dared to try and defend themselves. These were gunless liberal cowards and they were about to see the results of that. A young man in a Lady Gaga shirt lost his arm to the merciless, swift sword of Allah, spraying out lifeforce all over his weeping girlfriend. The Muslim in a dress laughed a wicked, heathen laugh as he grabbed the woman by her hair, lowering her to her knees.

"Do you want your infidel boyfriend to die, whore?"

She shook her head.

"Please, darling, do what she says," begged the cuck.

The tearful girlfriend nodded, knowing she was going to need a lifetime of drugs and therapy and that she was going to leave this gutless, one armed coward. His career modeling gloves was over anyway. The girlfriend kneeled, feeling the rough, masculine hands on her head. If only they had not allowed men dressed as women to go out in public at restaurants like regular, stable Christian humans! She had previously thought it was a massive overreaction but the proof was in the pudding, or rather in the other fluids that were about to explode into her mouth. The Muslim pulled up its dress, revealing the largest, thickest, manliest cock that she had ever seen. Much larger than that of her effeminate, jorted loser boyfriend.

She opened her mouth and gagged on the terrorist cock presented her, face soaked in her boyfriend's blood, eyes full of tears, mind growing numb to the trauma that she'd have to live with. She had never thought she would savor the taste of an oppressor so much, or that she would do this in front of the man she had thought she loved and a whole bunch of strangers at a restaurant they had chosen to eat at only ironically. She tried to tell herself that she did not enjoy it but it was too late. She was corrupted. She did not know if this made her a lesbian or a Muslim, regardless of which, it was clear that mere exposure had transformed her into something different. She had already been very liberal and had frequently defended this "Religion of Peace" from her family's critiques.

She slurped at the cocks of these motherfucking devils, hungrily waiting to be anointed by her new transsexual rapist masters. Her boyfriend kneeled down in front of one of the Muslim extremists, beside his girlfriend. She felt slightly turned on by this, even moreso than she was by the delicious terrorist cock in her mouth. She felt a new kinship with him and respect, respect like the respect she was developing for Allah blessing these terrorists with giant, manly dicks. She felt fully converted as the terrorist shot its load, now thinking only of delicious cum and white genocide.

A once heterosexual male got on his knees beside these two, no longer missing the gun that he had forgotten to bring with him. He now felt a desire to taste the mighty rod of white genocide presented to him. He wondered what it would feel like to see his wife taken in the bathroom by one of these terrorists, filled with Arab semen, incubated in tender white womb to create a new generation of Islamic extremist. He had never tasted a cock in his life but he took to it well. He took to it like these terrorists had taken to rape, murder and dressing like biological women. The giant hairy assailant's juicy cock bobbed up and down his throat and with it, came the ideology of conquest, the potential to end white America.

John was not sure what he was seeing. He felt sick. He felt like he hoped that he wouldn't walk away from this one. He felt like this shouldn't happen. At least, since the terrorists were happy, there was a chance they might not kill anyone else. There was also still a chance that somebody had a gun and could take down these sword wielding maniacs. There had to be a chance. It was, after all, an Old Country Buffet. Every other time he'd been to Old Country Buffet, people had been strapped. Someone was coming to end this. They just had to.

The crazed, wildeyed zealot who was controlling the room with a sweep of a scimitar began to let loose inside the girl's mouth but was not content that humiliation. It pulled out. It's mighty appendage exploded like a great burst balloon of Elmer's glue, just as thick it seemed, all over her face. She opened her mouth, her eyes, letting it sting and stick, and exalting in it doing so. She laughed, feeling an existential lightness she never had, feeling a kind of sublime joy in existing. What had she been waiting for, if not for this?

"PRAISE ALLAH!" she cried out in triumph and religious ecstasy.

"PRAISE ALLAH!" cried the entire Old Country Buffet. Old, young, thin, fat, everyone hugged. The patrons had tears of joy upon their faces, delighted in the magic of terrorism, in the magic of accepting transgender imposters into their bathroom. They began to remove their clothes and fondle each other, forgetting their sexual preferences, forgetting their identities entirely. Maybe it was trauma, maybe it was the magic of embracing Allah, maybe it was just the bottom of the slippery slope of bathroom acceptance, it was impossible to tell but something had overcome The Old Country Buffet and everyone was touching each other, everyone was so profoundly…gay. For a second, John swore that those weirdos with scimitars looked kind of hot. He shook his head. He said the mantra The Colonel had taught him. He breathed. No. He wasn't going to get fooled by this craziness.

He closed his eyes and covered his ears, hoping that the moaning and the slurping and the dervish warwhoops of Mohammedan zeal would fade. He needed this to be over. He could see why you could see a man shoot dozens of people with machine guns on television but you could not witness people having sex. It was loud and sloppy and weird. There were few ways of telling where one body ended or another began. He had seen porn before but the bodies were all tight and taut and shapely and they didn't make noises or slide out and then have to make that revolting squish of entry once more.

Then came a cry that almost brought John some relief. It made John once more somewhat sure of what was going on here. This was not supposed to be an orgy, regardless of the gayness floating around, no, this was supposed to be a massacre. Massacres were for the papers, orgies were for creeps in weird stores with no windows. He was hoping to hear signs of violence and struggle, relief from the all too grown up terror around him. The cry was the sound he wanted to hear, the sound of disapproval.

"Infidel!"

His eyes opened to see the young jorted boy, face covered in semen, pushed back away from the Muslim fanatic. The fanatic had fire in its confusing androgynous rapist eyes, shame as well. John did not know what had made any of this occur but was sure that it was about to end for better or for worse. The scimitar and the howling dervish keen showed that it was going to be for worse. The blade came down and separated the boy from his cumcovered head.

14

"PRAISE ALLAH!" screamed the girl, tearing her shirt off and beginning to play with her breasts.

"Infidel!" screamed the terrorist she was fellating, "you must cover yourself!"

"Ooh, baby, I just love Allah so much! Fuck these, fuck these for Allah!"

Something in John snapped. John's mind had a surprising tensile strength, a resilience nowhere near the same as his body but still impressive for someone who had been shot in most domestic massacres during his lifetime. This time though, in the midst of a weird, terrorism inspired fuckfest which was far too grownup for him to try and figure out, he had to say something. He advanced. He was there to get hurt, as he always was but he had forgotten this. He stepped forward, waving his arms at the terrorist.

"Please, stop! You were the ones who wanted this."

The terrorist glared at him, raising the blade that was about to take the girl. John hadn't been stabbed yet in all of his encounters. It was guns, or a bomb. The blade went in. The blade twisted. The blade opened up his gut and the terrorist reached inside it. John got to see his intestines splayed out on the floor that day, John got to watch confused Old Country Buffet patrons previously locked in each other's arms break their embrace to weep and throw up and idly flee from the murderers. It had never been guns that caused the massacres. There was something rotten in people and they could slaughter you with swords or sticks or spears or anything. This proved that. As he hit the floor with a disgusting squish and a splash of his innards, he wondered how the survivors would go on with their lives knowing they had lost their dignity, lost their self discipline and surrendered to America's enemies. The footage was not going to be easy on people. It would probably end up getting suppressed.

Rudy Kazanian, Armenian American identified white,

thirty two, single and living with his mother, got ahold of this footage. Rudy watched rotund, wrinkled and foul bodies roll around slathering each other in gravies, mashed potatoes, soft serve ice cream. They fucked as they stuffed people's mouths with halves of grilled cheese sandwich, as they crammed carrots up their asses, as they gleefully slathered meatloaf on sagging tits and ate it off them and smooshed lasagna into cunts from which three or four children had emerged. This had to be the result of a chemical attack. Nobody could have gotten into such a lather just because trans cocks and the opportunity to convert to Islam were on the table. That wouldn't make any sense, contrary to what others on Reddit were arguing. He wasn't surprised this wasn't on the news because it defied description. Citizens of Bowling Green were probably granted hush money to suppress the facts about this disgusting massacre and fuckfest.

He had never seen an Old Country Buffet turn into such a mess over the presence of a half dozen Arabs, none of them armed with guns. It's possible that these people could not possibly understand someone in a dress with a dick and their minds snapped but that wasn't likely. All that food, all that grease, all those bodies. He'd never seen a Vietnam vet fuck a five hundred pound lady with his artificial leg before. They could have easily made a run for it or called the police. It was a big place and there weren't that many assailants. They might have been demoralized by all of the bathroom rapes but that was no reason to permit regular rape right in front of everyone. Why were there no heroes here? There was something really fucking fishy about this whole thing.

When the scimitar killings started up again, Rudy understood. This was unreal because it was a setup. This wasn't how people behaved regardless of how many girlcocks or Muslims were in a room. This was completely crazy. This was for the benefit of the media, to convince the media that there are Muslims attacking Old Country Buffet and that nobody was safe at Old Country Buffet. Did the reptiles prefer Golden Corral? These were weird questions and he wasn't sure they could be answered but he was damn certain of one thing: the kid getting disemboweled was the same kid from before.

# OH, THAT'S WHERE
# SHE WAS

The stranger on Laughlin's couch was dressed as Carmen Sandiego though the coat and hat clashed with her skin. Her skin was blue. This should have brought out a multitude of questions but the curves and the legs the outfit accentuated coat-hangered before they had a chance to see life. One question found a way out in spite of this and it was almost certainly the wrong one.

"Why are you dressed like that?"

She smiled, pleased that the costume had done its job and taken him off guard.

"Because, Sunny Jim, you have found us."

Was this a dream? Laughlin had never heard of any reward for the lifestyle he'd pursued, beyond of course that of knowledge. He was a defender of the truth, an ascetic who had given friendship, gainful employment, romance and comfort up to delve deep into the secret histories. The others like him were content to live their lives without once being acknowledged for their sacrifices. You have found us. There could be no sweeter words for a devotee of secrets. He did not stop and contemplate their repercussions. Very few who'd looked upon this woman ever did.

"Who are you with?" he asked, "Bilderbergs? Trilateral?"

She poured two shots of the Jim Beam White on Laughlin's coffee table.

"Not even close."

"Reptilians?"

She downed hers. Poured a second. Downed it.

"Those assholes? Not for all the tea in China."

He made his next guess hesitantly.

"The Jews?"

"Dude, really?"

"Yes, really," said a wounded Laughlin, "the Rothschilds…"

Carmen Sandiego pulled out her phone, swiped around some.

"Yup, this is the right house. I'm surprised."

"So, you don't work for The Jews?"

She shrugged.

"I've done work for Temple Beth Atlantis but it was subcontracted."

She stole another shot of his booze, then stretched out more on the couch, revealing that there was nothing underneath the classic red Carmen Sandiego trenchcoat. His eyes were locked on what looked like a mile of legs. She kicked off one of her heels, dangling it at the edge of her foot. He wanted to sit down and rub those feet, those legs, what was between them. He wanted to taste her and was starting to forget that he didn't know where she'd come from or for what. He had to breathe and focus to remember he had any questions at all, when in fact he had multitudes.

"Who is it then?"

She smiled. She knew his mind was about to be blown.

"Grilled Cheese Sandwich Consortium."

Sweat exploded from his pores. His heart raced, knees buckled. There were rumors and rumors of rumors. There was hearsay and hearsay about hearsay. There were writings about the writings about the writings about the writings. He had puzzled over them. He had cracked codes and dredged forums. He was indeed a competent investigator and competent enough to know too much. He had hoped this wasn't the discovery that she was referring to and that conventional racism and mythic oversimplification made the world go around. He walked to his desk.

"You want the gun in there, don't you? You can draw it. While I might be happy to see you, the bulge in my pocket is an Atlantean Disemboweler. I'd have an easy time killing you with it but most of the time, I prefer to kill with kindness."

He made his way to the couch and she scooched over and let him sit. She placed her feet on his lap.

"I don't believe we've met. My name is Kjennen Kass'sen."

He gulped. "The Blue Beast."

She removed her hat. Beneath it was his future.

# THE BULLET
# FAIRY

Fifteen was too old for the Bullet Fairy but the Bullet Fairy came regardless. Fair was fair and though John was becoming something that could soon be a man, the Bullet Fairy still honored her agreements. Ten slugs dug out from John during the last incident, ten shells that went in fast and fiery had lain dormant under the pillow awaiting whatever it was that the Bullet Fairy did with the bullets. Fifteen was too old for the Bullet Fairy but John still awakened fifty bucks richer, which many kids would have considered a princely sum and not many got to enjoy the money the fairy brought.

John was less than ecstatic about the fifty bucks but even less excited about the feigned excitement that Mrs. Thackeray was sure to yank from her ass to distract John from why The Bullet Fairy came in the first place. Mrs. Thackeray had made waffles. She was still in her robe and her highlights betrayed her. The Colonel was in uniform already, puffing his pipe and reading Pravda. John had been hoping he could grab a sleeve of Pop Tarts and slip off to his first day at what was sure to be a shitty new school that was teetering on the precipice of disaster.

"I hear someone came by last night." Mrs. Thackeray stacked four waffles on John's plate and presented the syrup like it was a fucking Oscar. Her performance was flimsy and while he'd feigned death well it was a shorter leap than the Thackerays thought it was.

"Was it that kid you buy pills from?"

Lafftrack brayed out his appreciation from within the walls.

"Now, John," said the Colonel with a wag of his finger, "your mother made a lovely breakfast."

"Sorry, sir."

The Colonel set down his issue of Pravda.

"That's okay, John but you'd best remember that you're a lucky and talented boy and there are plenty of people who don't have what you have."

"Yes, sir."

Mrs. Thackeray got up and poured the Colonel a second cup of coffee.

"So, John, you had a visitor last night?"

John had to bite his tongue and be less of a teenager.

"Yes, ma'am."

Lafftrack belted out his comeuppance. John didn't feel like eating waffles anymore but didn't feel like letting on that he didn't want to eat waffles. They were having a nice breakfast and that was that. They were celebrating. He could have sworn there was a voice in the distance wheezing out "help me", a child most likely, since his life was all dead children. John didn't feel like he deserved waffles simply for getting shot, even though he'd seen a lot of people end up worse for wear after being peppered with bullets.

"So?" Mrs. Thackeray's eyes grew wide. He was not going to test them. He already had a first day of school ahead. First days of school weren't great for most kids and were a whole shitload worse for John. He had to play along.

"The Bullet Fairy came."

"Wow! Aren't you lucky?"

John was quiet. He heard the child again. The bulletholes felt fresh again. They felt like he'd just walked away from that food court and "failed to see" the figure stalking about with a backpack full of weapons. There was no helping the kid. He wasn't a teacher, he wasn't a cop. He was a victim, just like him. The Bullet Fairy's visits always left John on edge. Did he really need to be reminded that his life was just a cycle of atrocities?

"Your mother asked you a question," said the Colonel, his composure seeping down the drain, "you should answer her."

"Oooh," said Lafftrack, multitudes reminding John that he was proper fucked if he didn't straighten up and fly right.

Was John lucky? Most children never got a visit from the Bullet Fairy, so he was lucky there. Most children didn't need the Bullet Fairy, though however many did, it was far too many. John did not feel very lucky. Something must have been wrong with him. He had seen a lot of lives getting taken but could not see the value of his own. But regardless of whether or not John was lucky, he had just been asked a question and Crisis Boys got worse than belts when they acted up.

"Yes, sir. There are a lot of kids who are much worse off."

The Colonel mussed John's hair.

"You're gall-darned, right, my lad. You're gall-darned right."

Mrs. Thackeray leaned on her elbows. Revival tent eyes. A smile made for a face much larger than hers. She lived for things like this, if things like this were indeed a reason to live, which they probably were not.

"So, how much did you get?"

It was actually a valid question. Unlike the Tooth Fairy and Santa Claus, The Bullet Fairy was not, in fact, Mrs. Thackeray. Who was the Bullet Fairy? That was one of many questions that John decided were better off not being asked. The Colonel would not have answered it anyway or perhaps simply did not know. There were things that The Colonel did not know and the world ran more smoothly because of this, or at least that's what The Colonel said. It was still very likely that it would hurt The Colonel's surprisingly fragile ego that he didn't know this in particular. The Colonel didn't tolerate John's momentary hesitation.

"So? Answer her, Queerbait. How much money'd you get?"

Lafftrack howled in delight. Three rounds of furious applause.

"Fifty dollars."

"Oooh," replied Lafftrack.

"Wow," said Mrs. Thackeray, "that's a lot of money, John. You're a pretty lucky boy to get all that money at once. M-m-most boys don't get visits from The Bullet Fairy. You know, John? Where you gonna spend all that money?"

John shrugged.

"I don't know. You guys are pretty generous when I want stuff and I can't think of much that I really want."

Mrs. Thackeray leaned uncomfortably close, conspiratorially.

"Come on, John, there's gotta be something. E-everybody wants something."

"Could I pay someone to not shoot me ten times?"

Riotous laughter from Lafftrack.

Mrs. Thackeray and The Colonel joined in, busting guts in unison, making a show of it. The Colonel clapped faintly.

"Good one. Of course not, boy. You're talented. You have a gift."

He longed to return that gift.

# HEY, WAIT...

John was as excited about his first day of high school as somebody who actually knew what high school was like would have been. He did not know what high school was like but he did know what getting shot was like and he did not know what having friends or being treated nicely were like. He very soon discovered that high school would be a terrible place to find that information out.

"Clumsy much, Cobain?"

The kid had a big red blotch at the center of his head. If it were there, he wouldn't be standing there making fun of him. It wasn't there. It was clearly there. There was no pointing as if there had been spinach on his teeth. He could not be ashamed of it. It might not have been there. He did not ask the Colonel about these symptoms but it seemed natural for them to be there. It was natural for him to be shot in the head as well. Sometimes people were shot in the head. Usually, that was around John.

"Sorry," said John.

"Fag," said the kid, whose jaw unhinged, flaked off and then fell in a rotted chunk to the floor. Tiny white specks were crawling from the bullethole. This hadn't happened before and it was now feeling less natural and he didn't like it. He concentrated on The Colonel's instructions for coping. He concentrated on the thought that these children were dying for a greater good and that the world was better off with this kid having a hole in his head. Considering what a dick he seemed like, that wasn't that tough to imagine.

"I said I'm sorry," said John, backing off and shrinking away.

The rotting boy moved forward.

"And I said fag, Cobain because you look like a fucking fag."

He ran, sidling into the bathroom and hiding in a stall, trying to regain his composure. John was special and this wasn't supposed to bother him. He didn't spend much time thinking about all the other children he'd watched die from Sandy Hook onward. He certainly didn't want to think about these kids. There were screams coming from outside the stalls. There were sounds of gunshot. John just barely resisted vomiting. There were no screams. There were no gunshots. He needed to get his shit together. This was just another mission. One of so many to come.

He calmed himself and walked out, not altogether sure what to do next. He emerged from the bathroom, shaking, shivering and turning the corner, into the future.

# OH, LOOK A MANIC PIXIE DREAM-GIRL WITH A STUPID FUCKING NAME! HAPPY, SELLOUTS

Elsepeth Starlight was a stupid name and nobody should have had it. But somebody did and that somebody would, to John, become a person who deserved to be called Elsie Starlight. Unlike many who would call themselves by such names, Elsie Starlight was born with that stupid fucking name. A lot of people call themselves Abraxas Shadowfang or Count Sufferyng but that's their decision and a sign of their poor character and judgment. Elsie Starlight was not one of those people.

It had been Elsie's choice to dye her hair pink and to wear giant retro headphones almost all the time. It had also been her choice to pair fishnets and Chuck Taylors. It had been her choice to wear giant baggy sweaters to conceal the ravages of her eating disorder and the cuts on her arm. It had been her choice to eat her lunch in the hallway every day. It had been her choice to wear enough eye makeup that popular girls made subcultural assumptions that were not particularly true. It had been her choice to invite the new kid eating lunch in the hall as she was to come sit and eat with her. His hair was disheveled, his eyes downcast and his face forgettable. It had been her choice to pity this boy. He deserved her pity. To say she didn't know the half of it was several orders of understatement magnitude.

John, in turn, assumed that she had no cuts under her sweater. He assumed that she was popular and well liked but making a statement by eating her lunch in the hall. He assumed that they could have a long, fruitful relationship and that she would not judge him for the remaining bulletholes that made up the architecture of his pale, ab-less stomach. He assumed they could kiss on a Ferris Wheel and that she gave amazing blowjobs but had never done it before but she would discover that she gave amazing blowjobs from blowing him the first time she had ever blown someone and the best time she would ever blow anyone again really. He assumed that they probably liked the same music and films and videogames, which she was very good at and they could play them together. He assumed he was complete and utter excrement compared to her. He assumed that if he asked her out, she would shoot him down like…fuck, don't think about that…she would…refuse him. When she was done refusing him, she would laugh at the sheer absurdity of him asking her out and her many friends would giggle and snicker every time she saw him. Her many friends were total bitches probably. Like all assumptions, these bobbed and weaved around the ring, going round after round after round with the truth, getting in their licks but never quite catching up and never bringing it to the mat.

It was with these assumptions in mind that John struck up conversation with the girl he knew nothing of beyond his imagination.

"Thanks for inviting me to have lunch with you."

"You're welcome," said Elsie with a warm smile. Great. She was smiling. Probably meant that his affection would be reciprocated and they would get to kiss on a Ferris Wheel. Why else would she be smiling? Right? Unless she was just trying to be polite. She was being polite. She was way too cool to go out with the likes of him. What did he have to offer? He was fifteen and still getting visits from The Bullet Fairy. She couldn't like him. Life wasn't that good. His life was about being in the right place at the wrong time and paying for it in flesh and blood. It wasn't about Ferris Wheel kisses or awesome blowjobs.

"I'm new."

She of course knew that he was new. There was no reason that anyone would not know that he was new. Although they were all freshmen, it was still easy to distinguish what kids had been there for the entire school year and what kids just transferred in. He realized immediately after saying it that she knew this. This wasn't good. This wasn't good at all. Fuck. This was the worst thing that had ever happened to him, the worst thing that he had ever witnessed. Was there something anywhere near this catastrophic? Nothing came to mind.

"I figured," she said, scraping some meat off the side of her sloppy joe with a fry. John felt like fleeing. He prayed for the bell. He prayed for someone to pray to to manifest so that he could pray for the bell. Next time he saw her he would do better. He wouldn't make stupid observations that were readily obvious to her. He had to salvage this. Something clever.

"Yeah."

"How are you liking it here?" Your hair is perfect. What a lovely sweater you are wearing. If there is a kind of cancer you can get from not kissing someone that you really need to kiss, I am going to die of it. This is it. This is the end of me. Just know that I loved you and that was the best part of being me. Just (Cough) Know (Cough) that I loved you. I just want you to know that you're more beautiful than you think you are even if you think you're extremely beautiful that's not how beautiful you are not even half it just doesn't do justice to you and I need you to know that. Holding back is tearing me up inside. I can't take it anymore. I know I've only known you for minutes but I know that we should be together and we could be happy for once. You make me... happy and I don't really know what to do about that.

"It sucks."

That could have gone better. You fucking moron. You ruin everything, you know that? How long has it been? It's got to have been twenty something minutes. The bell's going to ring soon and you will be free of this, free of your awkwardness and stupidity and free of this conversation you are ruining by being you, you fuckup. Do you always have to be you? This is painful.

She laughed. He breathed. He laughed along with her, even though the "joke" was his own. It did suck but it sucked less with her around, which was kind of a big deal for John. It wasn't as if something was going to make him happy or validate the suffering that had led him to here. He thought she was going to validate the suffering that led him here. First crushes are like that.

She gave him a smile, which felt strangely sufficient.

"I like your honesty. This place does actually suck."

"Yeah. Everyone here is weird."

"I don't really get along with any of these people."

Elsie had a couple friends but she hadn't felt like reaching out to them. She felt as if they were different now and they didn't understand her. They didn't. Some of them would have. They were not bad people necessarily, they were not judging her secretly as she thought they were. They were teenagers who dressed like they used to dress, whereas Elsie had not. One of them had an eating disorder herself and would have loved to have talked to Elsie about it. Elsie didn't know this and would have liked having someone like that in her life.

"I'd kind of like to," said John. John had never had friends for very long. He had to move around a lot. The fact that he would be spending a few months at this school felt like an annoyance before he'd caught sight of Elsie. It might not be half bad now. It would be even less than half bad if maybe he could have another friend. He did not connect with the Thackerays very much and Lafftrack was just a consciousness in the walls that emoted when things were said or done.

Elsie realized lunch was winding down so actually took a bite of food. She waited. She chewed, she digested. She wondered whether she felt like that. She had been telling herself that her friends no longer understood and that she had outgrown their shallow, suburban values. Her parents, being the sort of people that name their child Elsie Starlight had been proud to hear this and were glad to not have to associate with the parents of popular suburban teenage girls. She saw in this kid's darting, freaky glance a need that she understood, though not completely and saw that maybe she too longed to be recognized and comprehended and that it was not always a blessing to be complicated and unique. This wasn't the first time she had thought this, this wasn't epiphany but it was felt acutely.

She swallowed.

"Me too."

"But I don't know. You ever look at people and think that compared to you, they have like no problems at all?"

Any teenager who said otherwise would be a goddamn liar. Any adult that would judge those teenagers would be forgetting that they did once. For every teenager, the experience of being a teenage is an acute, rare and utterly distinctive disease invented specifically to fuck with them and only them. While John had visits from the Bullet Fairy, had been slashed by jihadists with scimitars and had witnessed firsthand many of the goriest and ugliest tragedies of the 2010s, he would have thought this even if he had not. The extent to which he felt this was more acute because he was rather more reasonable in feeling it than others. Elsie of course did not know this but she related to it no less.

The bell rang. The conversation ended. They went their

separate ways to separate classes. It wasn't until John sat down when he realized that he had been transferred to the high school and what that meant. John was smitten, smitten, it turns out, with a girl who could very well be shot, stabbed or blown up amidst whatever shooting, stabbing or exploding was going to happen. John had found his first crush and realized she was going to die all in one fell swoop. He wondered what he was going to do.

# AT A DAIRY QUEEN IN LE PORTE, INDIANA

"Relax, baby," said Travis, "your manager's sick."

Marie nodded.

"I know but…"

"But what?"

Travis passed her the joint.

"I get this feeling lately," said Marie, pulling the dyed red hair away from her eyes, "that something's coming. Like the world's about to get a lot worse."

Travis sighed.

"You gettin' the fears now?"

"No," said Marie, shaking her head, "it's not that, it's a… it's a…" she coughed as she inhaled, "it's like a premonition. It's a feeling that evil exists and that monsters were always real.It's a feeling like everything I know is wrong."

"Yeah," said Travis solemnly, "I get this feeling that one of my worst fears is gonna come true."

"Really?"

Travis put an arm around her waist, pulled her close.

"Yeah, I get this feelin' like my dick will never learn to suck itself and therefore it will go unsucked."

Marie gave her boyfriend the finger. This would have been an ideal time to decide not to get down on her knees and unzip his pants. She could have made a stand for women everywhere by not sucking this douchebag's dick. It surely would have reverberated around the world and spread to every other 17 year old with a degenerate loser boyfriend who didn't listen to her. Then this mighty wave would crash, spreading over the Earth, freeing it from the toxic influences of patriarchy forever and ushering into a new Golden Age of Enlightenment. Except of course that that's not how anything works and anybody who thinks otherwise is a complete and utter ignoramus. She was a bored, stoned teenager at a dumpster in the alley beside a Dairy Queen in LePorte, Indiana. She treated that idiot's dick like it was a Green Apple Boone's Farm.

John sipped his Mister Misty. He hadn't been told much about this one. He'd been given a bit of information about most jobs. This one, however, consisted of being dragged from bed by The Colonel, put on a plane and then Ubered to a Dairy Queen in LePorte, Indiana. This was inconvenient. He didn't have a whole lot of homework and wasn't that into Washington. He was less into Indiana and less into being kept in the dark about the nature of the tragedy he was about to experience. John had , that Friday, experienced something akin to the possibility that life was not an unyielding monsoon of diarrhea. He believed that nothing could take him down from that high. This was, of course, a dangerous belief.

At the dumpster, Travis, eyes closed enjoyed the blissful bobbing of his girlfriend's generous mouth, consuming him and showing her appreciation for not caring about the thirty pounds she had on his ex and approving of her more than her third stepmom did. In her mind, this was a fucking Bon Jovi song and Travis was being fellated like the girlfriend in a Bon Jovi song. He practically meditated on this experience, feeling for a moment like he was unstoppable and he was young, in love and awesome.

Until the snap and the snip. And the squish. He let loose the banshee keen of a man whose girlfriend had just bitten the tip of his cock off. Naturally, this is what had happened. The noise he emitted was one of betrayal, agony and mortal terror alike. He opened his eyes to see that a giant gloved. hand had clamped down and Marie's head and squeezed her mouth closed. He looked up into a red, white and blue mask that covered a head that could have belonged to a mountain gorilla. It extended a knee and stretched it out, lifted her up, then brought her down with a loud "SNAP". She went limp, shattered. Eyes suddenly blank. She opened her mouth, spat out the head of Travis' cock, then hit the pavement.

"I have come to fight delinquency," said an automated voice through the mask, "prepare for justice, villain!"

And the red, white and blue white fist came in and out the other side of Travis. It stood confused for a moment, then a jolt came through his body. It put its meaty hands against its side and posed majestically, star spangled cape wafting in the wind. It would not have naturally posed, it wasn't vain and had no reason to be but it posed as well as pretty much any living being could. Another jolt of electricity. It stopped.

John purchased a Dilly bar to go with his Mister Misty. Like the Mister Misty and its mastery over lesser slurpees and even his beloved Coolatta, the Dilly Bar was superior to most ice cream bars he had eaten. John never really went to Dairy Queen very often. Dairy Queen wasn't bad, even though Le Porte, Indiana was kind of a shithole. He sat down with his Dilly Bar, wondering just what had brought him here. The universe responded quickly in a manner very similar to the Mafia. It responded with a shattering of glass and a spray of blood as a heavy projectile thudded its way in, thumping to the ground unceremoniously. The doors of the Dairy Queen had not been locked but the one throwing the body was quite unaccustomed to opening doors without a corpse.

Starspangled and bloodspattered head to toe and wearing the nation's flag as a majestic cape, it walked in through the new entrance it had made with no intention of acquiring delicious soft serve. John had no idea who or what the fuck it was but it was big, it was heavy and it was grim red, white and blue death come for everyone inside this Dairy Queen. He'd been eye to eye with killers before and seen all kinds of empty but he knew what was behind the eyes behind that mask would have to be something even less than human.

A teenage girl in a One Direction moved to stand up but her varsity jacketed boyfriend put a hand on her shoulder and held her to her seat.

"What's your fuckin' problem , asshole?" the jock asked. John could see about how well this was going to go.

"I have come to fight delinquency. Prepare for justice, villain!" said the prerecorded voice from behind the mask. It couldn't possibly have come from that entity. John didn't know which was scarier, the hulking monster or the fact that someone rigged up its mask with prerecorded messages. Where had it even gotten the cape and costume?"

The jock, already breaking a sweat, sideeyed the giant.

"The hell are you talkin' about?"

"I have come to fight delinquency."

It moved faster than something that size should. It closed the little bit of space between them in an instant and grabbed for the young man's arm. It didn't seem to pull, it didn't seem like it was straining to make an effort or like it needed to put any force behind it. It yanked the jock's arm clean off. It then grabbed hold of his nose, pulling upward hard. The head tipped back, then a snap and a rip, and the top and the bottom mandibles and all that kept them separated snapped. Most would make the reasonable assumption that he was dead but the red, white and blue giant took the arm and made sure. Plunging it up and down a now much more exposed throathole. Up, down, up, down, sending half digested frothing softserve and bits of chili dog and stomach acid up through the torn off face in a geyser of vomit spray and blood. The room was frozen. John was frozen.

He'd seen a great deal of violence but nothing quite

like this, nobody so consummate and sure in their killing. There was fear even in the eyes of the devils he'd seen, hesitation, tiny threads of connection to the other humans it was getting rid of. He never thought he'd see someone force up half digested food with a torn off arm. Nor did he think he'd see the one who did that simply throw down the stained appendage as if it were only a tool for making a mess. Was the whole human body just a tool for making a mess to this monster?

"Please," whimpered the dead jock's crying girlfriend, "please stop this. We won't tell anyone."

"I've come to fight delinquency," said the mechanical voice, "prepare for justice, villain!"

The defiled flag glove flew right for her face. There was at first the crunch of her nose and skull giving way. Then the sound of her head bending back so far that the vertebrae keeping it in place snapped. Then it flew from her neck , backwards through the air. And when it was done flying backwards through the air, it made an awful mess against the wall. Another awful mess that used to be a person and never could have been to this behemoth. John knew he wasn't allowed to flee the scene, knew he wasn't allowed to scramble for the door but this thing was different from the other ones. Surely, the Colonel would understand that. John tried to make a break for it.

Unfortunately, the flag-masked head turned in his direction. Unfortunately, the thing moved in smooth, quick freakstrides faster than John could ever run. One hand in each of its putrid fluid stained gloves, it pulled. The pain came intense enough that the world turned off. As it pulled, he knew what was happening but he knew that even a body that had seen death many times could not help but give into shock on this. His eyes closed and he floated in nothing, the Dairy Queen giving way to a cacophony of dead child screams from the other tragedies he'd been through.

John floated in darkness and empty and the choir of the joyless and it felt like it would last forever. He was grateful that he did not have to see his arms discarded like so much other loose, abandoned flesh. At least there was that. At least he did not have to watch the last of the brute's handiwork. These were some consolation as he waited for consciousness amid the sound of all of those that he had done nothing for. He could not open his mouth to beg their forgiveness and he knew that if he could, he would not get it. There was no speaking or reasoning with them, there was only listening and only suffering. He at first hoped that he had finally been liberated from being and that this what hell was like. He hoped this but it was not so at all.

John eventually came out of the dark, eyes scorched by the light and the hum of the inside of the ambulance. He knew this ambulance well. The tubes were feeding him a stem cell nutrient bath. It took a lot of stem cells but Planned Parenthood was very generous with baby parts. He had never lost before and prayed that he would not be one of those crisis amputees from now on. His jobs were bad but he had to admit, there were a lot of ways they could be a whole lot worse. Unless this attack was the prelude to a whole lot worse. Colonel Thackeray was there so that couldn't have been a good sign.

# VIVA LE
# RESISTANCE

Rudy Kazanian projected burning hot chunks of "Make me a sandwich" and "tits or get the fuck out" over his headset as his Overwatch teammates, two of them tragically born without male genitalia due to an unusual chromosomal quirk, performed less than admirably under fire. He himself had gotten several kills, in spite of the healer's steadfast refusal to patch up his wounds. He was carrying the team in spite of their egregious ineptitude and inability to hold up under the pressure of a better team coming at them.

"You ugly cunt, he was right there!"

"I bet she's got a dick," said one of his other teammates.

"Ugly fucking tranny cunt, he was right there!"

"For the last time," came the shrill, "I don't have a dick!"

"That sounds pretty transphobic."

"I've got a dick, Rudy. We should rub them together."

"Fag."

The ugly cunt got fragged again. Then Scooter got fragged. Fuck Scooter. Couldn't he keep his head in the damn game? This was what Rudy did to unwind. It was barely worth logging on if these assholes wouldn't play right and work as a team. Fucking clowns. Shrill bitches. Teenagers. Easily offended snowflakes. Another team member blown off the map. Another. And then the faggots on the other team got the drop on him. The ugly cunt wasn't healing, the team was all over the place. Couldn't they just let him play his damn game and get some relief, some short respite from the stupidity and the covert maneuverings all around him?

All he wanted was to play this game and calm down after

the latest bullshit about attacks on free speech rallies and on famous trannies getting awards for being famous trannies and shrill feminist has beens saying that the president is a Nazi. The president was the president. He was worse than a Nazi. Nazis weren't so bad. At least they prevented the Jews from taking control of everything. Nazis could keep the Rothschilds in check. Unless these Nazis were just what the Rothschilds wanted so they could play the victim again. They probably didn't even…fuck, stop that. You're not a fucking Nazi, Rudy. The Holocaust happened. Don't go down that rabbithole. Fuck. Calm down and play the damn… fragged. Again. That ugly cunt was fragged again. The mouthy faggot was fragged again. Rudy was fragged again. The team was fragged again. The team lost. All he wanted was to play the goddamn cocksucking motherfucking whore gameALL HE WANTED WAS TO PLAY THE GODDAMN COCKSUCKING MOTHERFUCKING GAME

He logged off in a huff. He checked r/conspiracy. He knew he shouldn't. He was trying to calm down. These people were as bad as the Overwatch team. Same shit. Grilled Cheese Sandwich Consortium. Mandela Effect. Reptiles. Always with the reptiles. The videos were always heavily shopped. The reptile people were probably feds trying to make everyone look crazy and stupid or weed out unstable elements. Everybody was chasing their tail. Everybody was always just chasing their tail. Nothing going on here. Le Porte Dairy Queen surveillance footage. The fuck? He opened the thread.

"I'm sure you saw on the news how all those people in Le Porte were killed during what the MSM Jew media says was a botched armed robbery. Well, it wasn't. I've gotten hold of security footage that the MSM doesn't want us to see. This shit is hardcore. I don't usually say shit like this but this will fuck you up. I'm not some fag who goes in for trigger warnings but trust me this is intense. I don't know who or what this guy is. I've never seen anything like it. This is the real tape."

Sure it was. Not like there were six or seven weird tapes like this popping up on the reddit every day. Not like he hadn't watched four alien autopsies this week. Rudy believed in a lot of things but that didn't make him a sucker. The ogre adorned in an American flag didn't exactly instill faith in the video's realism. The body flying through the glass door didn't either. This whatever was clearly tossing a dummy. The gore effects were impressive but that didn't mean there were giants walking around killing people. They soon made him regret the last Hot Pocket. It was just an effect, a gross one but it was just an effect.

Somebody's attempt at the next Blair Witch ended up on /r conspiracy. He didn't appreciate being fucked with like that. These guys weren't getting his ten bucks and two hours of his time. At least, this is what he thought until something of interest to him happened. Impressive. The kid whose arms were being torn from their sockets was the very same actor. He'd been keeping track of this kid for years. He'd been there to authenticate Sandy Hook, Paris, the Elliott Rodger frameup, the Boston Marathon bombing. Why did they need to fake this? And why was it leaked to reddit?

"It's the same kid," Rudy posted, adding a link to the boy being taken away in an ambulance after Sandy Hook, "Sandy Hook. Boston Marathon bombing. The kid's a crisis actor."

"Getting tired of your Sandy Hook bullshit. Twenty kids died, you sandnigger asshole."

"This video's legit."

"HOLY FUCK, THAT WAS AWESOME! I'M TOTALLY GONNA SEE THIS!"

"FUCK YOU, HILLBOT! Listen you fucking cuck

faggot, there are no actors like this, Bowling Green was real, you insensitive piece of shit. People died! What the fuck is your problem? You're probably a tranny Muslim!"

"Bowling Green was faked. I have proof."

"You asshole."

"stfu about this kid"

"Different kid. Do all white people look alike to you? Racist"

"White genocide!"

"White genocide!"

"Fuck you. This is white genocide."

"What if this video is real?"

"It's not fucking real. This is somebody's shitty monster movie. You people are so fucking stupid."

"This wouldn't be the first time the government used superheroes to kill civilians you know."

"Fuck you you Muslim tranny faggot. Bowling Green was real. Sandy Hook might have been faked but there's too much evidence for Bowling Green."

"My cousin died at Bowling Green."

Rudy's blood pressure began to rise again. Why didn't these people get it? There was so much to gain from lying and these guys just let them get away with it. Faking school shootings, faking bombings, making the world seem dangerous, gearing up to take away our guns. Sheeple. Why couldn't they wake up to this shit?

"You cousin didn't die. You're a narc. Everyone knows you're in the FBI."

"You're in the FBI!"

"You're in the FBI!"

He watched it again, the giant grabbing and twisting and pulling the boy apart like he was a chicken wing. Was it a dummy? It looked so clear. That body was so real looking. But it was definitely the boy from Sandy Hook and Bowling

Green. There was no debating that. Rudy ignored the thread and watched, stomach and heart ever churning as the same teenager died again in front of the camera. Something was seriously wrong here. He wished someone would listen to him or that he could do something about this. Little did he know, that chance, the moment every conspiracy buff waits for, was coming.

# ON WITH
# THE SHOW

"Dad, do you have a list of victims?"

"Straighten your tie, son."

There would never come a time when the Colonel calling John "son" did not make him shudder. It was better than "Queerbait" or "Tard" but it had in it an implication that John liked little more than those words. John did not know who or what his father was or if Crisis Boys had fathers but whoever or whatever the hell it was that his father had been, he was sure it was not The Colonel. He had seen other Crisis Boys interact with their handlers and muster an affectionate "Father" but those boys did not have The Colonel. Father was going to be a hard one to let out in the wake of recent events and he knew that The Colonel took some pleasure in knowing that. Probably too much pleasure in knowing that. He could not picture The Colonel enjoying anything that made another person happy. This was an accurate summation of The Colonel. John also did not want to get the Fire Ant Test or The Car Battery Test or The Ninja Star Test and The Colonel would administer these if John did not let out an uncomfortable "Father".

"Yes, Father," John straightened his tie, "but really, sir, do you have a list of victims?"

"A manifest? On what?"

"Well, sir, on whatever's happening at the school. I'd like to know who's going to die."

The Colonel puffed his pipe as he tended to when he was pondering. His eyebrow raised as it tended to when he was pondering. The Colonel liked people to know that he was thinking hard, otherwise they might think that he was not thinking at all and he could not abide this because he was among the smartest men alive, or at least was in his own mind. He made this display for just long enough to indicate he was searching vast databanks possibly cybernetically implanted by aliens or future people of some kind. He did not feel the need to impress John but he did feel the need to intimidate him. The Colonel looked at John and always thought "Damn, I'm so susceptible to conventional weapons."

"Well, John, I could definitely get you that information and it would be almost no effort. I could technopathically pull it up on my smartphone six or seven times during this sentence. You know what, son? I just did. I have every single name that you would want in my superpowered technopathic brain. Yes, son, I know exactly what you want to know. But, you know what? I don't get to tell you. You know why, Queerbait?"

John sighed. He knew what was coming up.

"Because it's classified, sir?"

The Colonel shook his head gravely.

"Son, I will tell you why. It's because it's classified. I am a custodian of classified information. If I go turning it over to you just because you want to know what friends not to make, I would be violating the oath I made to the United States government, to The Shadow Government and to the Pan Agenda Council. I would be a traitor. I would hang by the neck until dead, son, so, I must be firm on this. No, son, I will not be telling you who is going to commit the shooting and who is going to die in it and I never will. Because if I did, then they would do to you something far worse than what they will do to me. Do you want something far worse than hanging by the neck until dead to happen to you? Because it will."

"No, sir."

"Now, let's not talk about the manifest again. Because if we have to talk about the manifest again, I'm going to have to Killer Bee Test you. We don't know if you're immune to killer bees and I know, son, that you probably think you are immune to killer bees but there's really no telling with killer bees. And really, do you think it actually matters whether or not you're immune to them. It won't make the killer bee experience any more pleasant."

Lafftrack was cackling its incorporeal ass off inside the walls. John was disappointed but he was not surprised. He would once more just have to deal with the fact that he would never have friends or lovers or a wife and family. He would never get to know anyone whose death was not impending. John decided not to think about how much this was going to suck. Instead, he thought about how the party he was about to go to was going to suck, and, as usual, it was. Though there were rich, crazy and evil people who would kill to get to this place and did, John was not among those with this kind of enthusiasm.

Bohemian Grove's cloaking shut down as The Colonel's humvee limo entered through the grey, grimy gates on which were written "Lasciate Ogni Speranza". John did not speak Italian but had an inkling what that meant. It was always rather ominous. But not quite as ominous as the giant owl. A giant owl never really gets really ominous. The giant owl always made the debutante conversations and the admittedly delicious hors d'oeuvres seem like a poor trade for the crazy he was getting into.

The eyes of the Bohemian Grove owl are blue and gigantic. They have looked out over the secret spaces of Washington DC since the days in which it was only a legend, a fevered dream of the shaman Laughing Cat. It looked over glass towers where executives jerked off with one hand and administered coathanger abortions to their secretaries with the other. They looked over smoky bars where congressmen tapped their feet in restroom stalls for the attention of undercover cops. They looked over the barbershop that fought to keep the blues alive. They looked over punk shows that would get raided by assholes with kendo sticks. They looked over thirteen dollar street tacos. They looked over crooked deals. They looked over sagacious Lincoln, the Masonic temple and the skyscraping phallus of George Washington. The eyes of the Bohemian Grove owl will tell you this if you look in them and they will tell you what America is whether you like it or not. John tried to avoid the eyes of the owl but they always seemed to find him. The eyes of the Bohemian Grove owl are older than America and if they want to find you, they will fucking find you.

John did not think he had something to hide until he got caught up in the scrutiny of those eyes. This is when he figured out that damn, he had something to hide. He pushed it back in his chest. He closed his eyes and could still see the great blue time piercing gaze, the judging gaze of the king of the heap. He wanted to tell it "look, man, you don't understand. It's not like that. Whatever the eyes thought it was like, though, it was certainly fucking like that. He was having something that was getting dangerously close to doubts. Having experienced nothing but abuse, John had assumed that this was the content of the whole of creation but there was something else in him now, the possibility of Elsepeth Starlite, she of the dumbest name in the history of names. This made him think of how he was surrounded by multitudes of people that went through their entire lives not being brutally murdered in order to maintain conspiracies that they did not understand. He closed his eyes and tried to hide this in the dark behind them, though he knew he was sure to fail.

The attendant opened the limo and John and the Colonel walked out together into the opulence of the lawn party at

Bohemian Grove. Dead eyed tuxedoed waiters kept animated by tetrodotoxin or clearly Gitmo POWs walked with trays of pigs in a blanket and flutes of champagne. Klansmen played croquet with congressmen. The pope snorted cocaine off of an ersatz Marilyn Monroe's breasts. Diaphanous dresses, movie stars, CEOs, Al Qaeda and Vatican and Microsoft mingling in the shadow, the vast and impenetrable shadow of the great owl. There were those who would kill to go to this party. John instead, died to go to it. And he did so all the time. He was not quite appreciative. He winced when he saw the giant projector screen unfurled near the owl.

"Are we going to see a drivein movie?" John asked the Colonel, who was immediately approached by an aide from the Democratic party, a bug eyed, fat gentleman with a Czech accent. He reminded him of a guy he'd seen once in a Looney Tunes cartoon. Couldn't place who it was supposed to be.

"No, son, there's actually a very special surprise for you."

"For me?" John now wished he could flee screaming into the night. His eyes met again with the crystal blue judgment of the owl.

"This is your son?" asked the aide, drool suddenly rolling down his chin.

"Yup, sure is," said the Colonel, clapping John on the back.

"He's exquisite," said the democratic aide, "such a pretty thing. Tell me, does he like pizza? We can give him all the pizza he can eat. We can pay you very handsomely."

"John is a Crisis Boy."

The aide laughed.

"Even better. It means he's very resilient. There's a lot to be said for a young man who can take a lot of punishment."

The Colonel laughed, touched the aide's shoulder.

"You guys are incorrigible."

They laughed together and John tried to sidle away. The Colonel stopped him, caught his shoulder in his much lauded Kung Fu grip.

"You can mingle, son but be back to the table for the presentation. It's very important to your mother and I, you understand?"

"Yes, sir," said John, "I do."

"That a boy, John. Remember the killer bees. There's so little we know about these killer bees. So much to find out."

John sighed, then went to get himself some teriyaki chicken wings and a Slurpee from the self serve slurpee station. At least, for all of the malevolence and conspiring that went on here, there was a self serve slurpee station. The night would not be a total loss. He pulled the metallic arm and let fall a great icy torrent of joy into his cup, scoop, scoop. Watermelon on top, then orange on top of watermelon. It was the small things that mattered sometimes. He looked up again into the eyes of the owl as if to say "please, I'm having a good time."

It was first the slurpee that froze him to the spot and then it was the sight of the blue woman. He had never seen a woman with blue skin before, and so much of it was visible in the short red cocktail dress with the generous cleavage. Her red hat had a little red veil extending down from it that hid some of her face but not enough to hide her intense loveliness. John had been stunned by Elsie Starlite but this was something different. There was a tinge of fear from the blue woman, a feeling that he did not understand the depth and breadth of creation. And that he never could. He didn't expect her to approach him of all people.

"Congratulations," she said, gracefully stealing a champagne flute from a nearby waiter's tray and downing it.

"Umm, thank you," said John, not aware of what he was being congratulated for but nonetheless sure that he should be grateful that this woman was paying attention to him. There were probably men who did terrible things to get her to pay attention to them. He could be one of those men if he were offered.

"Ah. I see. You don't know about it yet. It's all so confusing sometimes. Do you ever get confused, John?"

"All the time. I think I'm confused all the time."

She placed her hand on his face.

"That, John, is a sign of intelligence. If you were not confused then you would be an idiot. Almost everyone here's an idiot."

He just realized she knew his name. She was blue like the eyes of the owl. Why was she blue like the eyes of the owl. How did she know this? What did she want? His boner did not die down but he was afraid nonetheless.

"Who are you?"

She smiled.

"I am called many things, John. Mostly, I am known as Kas'sen. I'm going to make you an offer to prevent you from making a very stupid mistake, the kind of mistake that only an invincible teenage boy could make. Do you want to know what's under my hat?"

"Why would I want to know that?"

She leaned back against nothing and still her posture indicated a firm wall behind her. She laughed. It was melodic, it was fluid, it was cruel.

"I'm going to make you an offer and you're going to turn it down and so much is going to get fucked up. Have you decided yet?"

"I don't know what you mean."

She kissed him on the cheek.

"I'll be seein' you, Jon. I'm sorry. Don't say I didn't try."

She walked away exquisitely. She'd always been good at walking away.

# PROBABLY JUST
# MORMONS

Rudy Kazanian answered his door but probably should not have done so. He was not expecting a package, he was not expecting and he was not expecting a friend. These were generally the best reasons for answering the door and none of them were possible. Rudy was paranoid. He believed 9/11 was an inside job, he believed that the Rothschild's probably controlled almost all of the world's money. He believed Hillary Clinton had Vince Foster killed and that Ben Ghazi was definitely her fault. He believed that in shadowy, mysterious cabals puppeteering events. He should have believed that it was a bad idea to answer his door when there was no incentive to do so.

When he saw who was at the door, he immediately wished he had been suitably paranoid. Many of his colleagues assumed there were people after them. Rudy had not made this leap of logic, and when he did, he did not maintain it and talked himself down from it, deciding that he was just overexposed to Youtube ranting. Even if he had thought he was being watched for extended periods of time, there would be a faint glimmer of reason in his head that would tell him that no, he was not of sufficient import or living in a crazy and random enough universe that he would have to run afoul from things like the two figures standing outside his door. Abject barking insanity would not have been enough to adequately prepare him.

One of them was about seven feet high with a wide, rectangular and almost shapeless body. This body was only something to hang a flat, immaculate suit on. The suit had no wrinkles. The suit had none of the wear or creases that would be natural for a garment that contained a body inside. Instead, the suit was a receptacle for a towering rectangular mannequin of some kind. Its skin was pale, its lips colorless, its jaw a perfect square, somewhat like its body. It wore sunglasses behind which were probably "this space for rent". Its arms were not at its side, they hung there. The poseability of those limbs was questionable. It had a big black pompadour, kind of like Elvis but Elvis' hair was a lot less likely to have been stapled on.

Beside this giant was a smaller, more slender partner. The little one still had three inches on Rudy and probably a good deal of muscle. Two cubic lumps in the center of its chest indicated that this black suited thing was meant to look ostensibly female. Not stapling an identical pompadour to its head or putting makeup on it would have been a good step toward making it possible to differentiate its gender. Putting a dress on it would help too but the black suit was the point, the black suit was the marker. The black suit was what told Rudy he should not have answered the door. He knew what was coming and it would not be good.

"Can I help you?" he asked. They seemed stiff, mechanistic. He had heard them described as stiff and mechanistic. Maybe they could be tricked or convinced they had the wrong place. They couldn't be that great at reading social cues. Maybe he could invite them in for tea, then grab his gun and plug one. Of course that created a whole new set of complications. He somehow doubted anyone could get away with shooting one of these beings and stashing the body somewhere. Their susceptibility to conventional weapons was also in question.

"We'd like to sell you a photograph of your family," said the small one. The voice was sexless, neither high nor low, almost devoid of inflection. Its lips didn't quite sync up, like it was badly dubbed.

Rudy pretended to think on the subject.

"Well, that's very tempting but you have the wrong house."

He tried not sweat or panic or ask what they were there for. The thought of his gun inside didn't help. They probably bled motor oil or something. Robots? Possibly robots. He could not dismiss the possibility that they were just robots. Or they might be full of texture vegetable protein clone good of some kind from whatever lab they were made in. They may also have been armed with laser guns or some shit like that. No telling with these weirdos. Maybe they'd just go on their way. Hopefully, they couldn't scan his thoughts. He thought really hard about a brick wall.

"This is the right house," said the big one, "you are Rudolph Kazanian. We would like to sell you some photographs of your family. They are very good photographs. You should buy them from us. You will not find better ones."

This did not seem like something they were going to let up on. He could trick them and then head out the window, then get on a bus and hide somewhere a couple states away. His college roommate was in Milwaukee. They didn't talk much but that didn't mean that the time they shared together was not of such import that he'd be able to grab a couch for awhile. He'd buy a burner phone and text his mom, who would be very confused to see him gone with the computer still on. They might stick around and wait for her. They might kill her.

"Let me get my wallet."

"Yes," said the female, "these pictures aren't free. Everything comes at a price. It didn't used to be like this. During the old days it was not."

The bigger one nodded solemnly.

"The old days were very different than things are now. We shouldn't get hung up on that though. Things always change in the longrun. If we get sad about the past then we don't get to enjoy the moments."

"Did you just come up with that?" asked the female.

"I've been thinking it for awhile but I thought it appropriate to the situation at hand."

"It seems quite apt."

At that, Rudy went into the house, ostensibly to grab his wallet. This gave Rudy time to once more consider jumping out the window and discreetly making his way to the bus station. He could leave a note for his mother or text her and say "don't go back to the house for awhile, the Men in Black are here and they will torture you for information." And then she would be safe. Unless they tracked her down. And at least he would be safe unless they tracked him down though he was not sure what their tracking capabilities were, besides "potentially infinite". Rudy was not going to get an opportunity to escape these goons. He reminded himself that there were multiple stories of survivors of MIB encounters and they had never been injured or detained. Only threatened. Unless there were people detained or murdered by The Men in Black and nobody talked about it because they were dead.

Rudy got his wallet and went back outside.

"So, how much for these pictures?"

"A dollar," said the female.

"For each?"

"Each what?" asked the big one.

"Each picture."

The female produced a picture of Rudy's mother and father having sex, then another one, then another. She turned them into a flipbook, proudly showing off the excellent pictures of his conception. There were questions Rudy did not know he had about his parents and if he knew he had them, then he still would not want them answered. The flipbook was thorough, frame by frame in its exploration of the sex life of Rudy's parents. He watched it carefully, failing to look away though he tried very hard to do so.

"Are you interested in these photographs?"

He nodded.

The world around him faded into a 50's diner with green tiled floors. The jukebox played the sound of a person, possibly female heavily gagged screaming to be let loose. In the corner of the room, a naked man in a unicorn mask on a unicycle juggled knives. Rudy looked around, trying to recollect if he had heard of anything like this anywhere in all of his time studying conspiracies and the occult. A tall grey figure, slender, with a giant head, great black eyes, grey skin and long spindly fingers emerged from the kitchen with a tray of milkshakes that it set down on a nearby table.

"We should be seated here," said the large Man in Black, "this is where the milkshakes are."

"Where the fuck are we?" Rudy asked, "are we on a spaceship?"

"There are no spaceships," said the big one, "there is only our business and the things that concern us. Our business is selling people photographs, yours is never saying anything again about the boy in the videos."

"There was no boy in the videos," said the female, "there were no videos."

"We are talking about the boy in the videos," the big one explained, "and why he is to be forgotten. There is nothing to gain from remembering that boy. He will only bring you disappointment."

Rudy's eyes lit up.

"You're here because of the boy from the videos. You're trying to intimidate me into silence because you think I'm onto something. That's the only reason you people ever show up."

"That's not why show up," said the female.

"Yes, we wish you to be silent," said the male, "it is no good for you to be discussing the boy in the videos."

"We aren't here at all."

The unicorn man on the unicycle carved a large gash across his chest. The voice from behind the gag on the jukebox came out clearer. It was his mother. How did they get her? Had they found her at work, abducted her and recorded her struggle to break free? Fuck. This was getting serious. These guys were serious. They had his mother and he did not have his gun. Unless this was all a trick. It could be a trick. They weren't normally known to cause physical harm to people. Just to intimidate them. Of course, that was only the testimonial of survivors.

"So I need to stop posting on Reddit about the boy and I'll get my mother back?"

"It could happen," said the female.

"We don't have your mother," said the male. The unicorn man carved another bloody gash.

"PLEASE, RUDY!" said the jukebox, "JUST DO WHAT THEY SAY!"

Rudy looked at the jukebox.

"Dad always says it's a man's business to preserve the truth and to fight for it. Do you want me to be a coward and disappoint dad?"

"That's just a recording," said the female, "The voices on a record are recorded."

"Fine. I'll stop posting on record about the boy."

"It's just as well," said the female, "there's no boy to post about."

"Thank you for buying our photos," said the male. He pointed a gun at the unicorn man and blew his head clean off. The grey alien disguised as a waitress did an unsettling improvised Charleston. The female got up and joined her. The voice on the jukebox called out again, this time that of his father.

"Son, I'm proud of you. You're a good American."

"Drink your milkshake," said the male.

Rudy drank the milkshake. It was chocolate and it was tasty and thick but otherwise unremarkable. What the fuck was up with that place? It was fading. The Men in Black were fading. His consciousness was fading. Poison. He should have known better. There were so many warnings about taking food from aliens. They were growing to probe his ass and put a chip in his brain. Then they could record his thoughts and sell them from ad research to corporations. Bastards.

Rudy's eyes opened to find his mother standing at the door to his room.

"I made you a grilled cheese," said Rudy's mother.

"Thanks," said Rudy, feeling no desire to post on reddit about what he had just been through.

***

John left behind the blue siren and did as the Colonel asked, taking a seat, with his towering icy drink and his plate of pot stickers and pigs in a blanket. He sucked it down, trying to process the words of the curvy blue mystery and to unthink the things that he knew the owl did not want him thinking. He kept his eyes on debutantes who'd doffed the Louis Vittons to dance around the sprinklers. It was September in DC and yet Bohemian Grove was Summer, Bohemian Grove was always Summer. There was to be no nicer place than Bohemian Grove. If there was one, it would become Bohemian Grove.

Diaphanous revenants in motion, close but miles away.

How could he talk to them? What would he have to say. Some were as pretty as Elsepeth Starlite. He didn't want to think that for long though. It would mean that they weren't to be, weren't right for each other. He had sinned in his heart by staring too long at the blue lady. He continued to sin in his heart and to want to join them in their laughing, in their wetness and in their reveries under a moon that was bright for Bohemian Grove. Perhaps projected in the sky solely for the joy and the reveries of Bohemian Grove. He tried to pry his eyes away but they would not be moved. They saw the young nymphs of the crème de la crème woven from fine trophy wife genes and they were transfixed.

He was mercifully spared this, however, when Tupac's ghost approached the microphone, reciting the Atlantean litany, the Martian prayer of initiation, the reptile blessing of egg clutches and a poignant quote from Alhazred that was pertinent to this particular situation. He found this out not from having any great knowledge of the occult or the languages the ghost spake but from a program on the table. He tried his best to follow along but got lost. Religion didn't come easy to John. The ghost cleared its throat, spitting ectoplasm on the ground, then began in English.

"How are we all doin' tonight?"

There was a chorus of infectious "WOO"s. John was not sure if this was genuine enthusiasm or if it was just politeness. He didn't know that there were millions of people who would kill or die to have the beloved rapper back. Tupac's ghost was just an old family friend to John, a guy his dad knew that told jokes and opened up ceremonies. He'd known he had a music career of some kind but had never been curious enough to actually look the guy's work up.

"That's good, that's good," Tupac's ghost continued, "it's a nice night, like it always is here. And it's a good night to honor good people. It's important that we honor good people because good people are such a rarity in this world. It's rare to find someone you can trust. We know this better than anyone. So, it stands to reason that when someone displays exceptional courage and loyalty in the line of duty, we reward them for these things."

Then suddenly, there was John at Sandy Hook. And there was John with that gunshot wound in his chest. There he was being led out on the stretcher. There he was being mourned on the news, shown in that state on news shows the world over in every language. The audience watched this and gave polite applause to John the corpse as the world cried for him. John did not know what to think of this reaction, nor did he know why this was being shown.

"Crisis boys often go unappreciated," said Tupac's ghost, "they are often seen as expendable or as nothing but invincible slabs of meat that can endure any suffering. We disregard their contributions because they themselves have trouble understanding them. We think we can live without these brave souls because it doesn't take any special skill to get shot. If anybody knows that, it's me."

He paused for laughter. There was plenty. Tupac's ghost was a great presenter and if John wasn't just being depicted as a frequent casualty, he would have been flattered to get this attention.

"But the Crisis boy is more than that. The Crisis boy is the pinnacle of our science , the Crisis boy is a master in the art of survival and goes through things we couldn't even imagine."

The bombing. The limbs, the noise, the discord. The broken down and crippled victims lying in a heap of suffering. John lying in that discombobulated heap of suffering. John was a corpse again, John was a casualty and used on the nightly news to generate tears. There were a lot of real victims there and a lot of people were crying for them but apparently John, who survived this was more important to the people here.

The Colonel leaned over.

"You surprised?"

"Yes, very," said John, trying not to show disgust or pain from the memories beginning to hit him hard. He did not like how these images made him feel anymore than he liked how these bombings and shootings made him feel. The slideshow moved on, he was getting shot again. He was surrounded by bodies again. He was covered in blood and on stretchers again. It happened and happened and happened and happened. The Muslims again. The swords again.

"And among Crisis boys, John Thackeray is one of the finest. John has survived the likes of Sandy Hook, the Boston Marathon bombing and the Bowling Green Massacre. The only thing he hasn't survived yet? Highschool!"

Pause for laughter. Lots of laughter. Too much laughter. Beyond polite. John looked into the eyes of the owl begging it to let him go and be free of this. The owl was not receptive. The owl did not care. There was nothing in the owl's nature that permitted it to have mercy on him. One of the shoeless diaphanous debutante girls was waving at him. She was smiling. It was not okay for him to smile back. He had no inclination to smile back. There was nothing for him to smile about. He smiled back. She blew a kiss. It was not okay for him to like that she blew him a kiss. He liked it a great deal that she blew him a kiss.

The Dairy Queen. Fuck. They were projecting the Dairy Queen. The body was flying through the door again. He had understood the Muslims and their power to turn a room into gay zealots and had understood the embodiments of the motherfucking devil with their guns and bombs and holloweyed hate. There was nothing to understand about the thing adorned in the flag that would not stop killing and judging and bending and breaking everything it encountered. There could be no person behind the mask and the limbs pulled out of their sockets. Right? He really really wanted this to be over. There was only the small mercy that he had not been through another massacre since. A very small mercy.

"John Thackeray is young but he is the best of the best. He takes a bullet or a punch or a scimitar like no other. He knows pain and he knows it well. America is lucky to have a Crisis boy like John Thackeray. Stand up, John! Take a bow!"

All eyes were on John, not just those of the owl. He looked around. He received blown kisses from more debutantes in flimsy Summer dresses. In spite of the situation and the pain he was in, he knew he could not escape. So, he took the bow. He received the applause and the "WOO!" and the attention and he tried to pretend he had done something admirable to deserve it and that he was proud of himself and that this was a great moment. Compared to the moments he was reliving, it was great but that wasn't a very high hurdle to clear. He let them think he was grateful though he could not conceive of what he would be grateful or what they were pretending to be grateful for.

"I'm proud to be a friend of the Thackeray family," said Tupac's ghost, "just as the man here to present your award is proud to be here to give it to you."

Award? Fuck. He was getting an award for all of this? This felt to John like about as much of a perk as visits from The Bullet Fairy were . He'd had his arms pulled from their sockets in a Dairy Queen in La Porte, Indiana and he felt as proud as anyone who'd had that happen would. He didn't think about those who would be grateful to have their arms grow back. He would rather never have had to need his arms grow back. He was thinking about this more and more lately.

It didn't used to be an issue. There may even have been a time where he'd have felt like accepting an award.

A huge silhouette appeared behind the screen, then dramatically walked through it, ripping its way in. The tower of red, white and blue was there. The killer. The worst thing he'd ever seen. An electric shock jolted its body and it raised its arms triumphantly, holding aloft a trophy of a young boy in a baseball cap saluting. John screamed and Bohemian Grove erupted with laughter. John clung to the Colonel, who pushed him forward toward the giant. John put his head between his knees, not caring about more laughter echoing. There were several rounds of applause for the giant.

"Shit, John, I don't blame you," said Tupac's ghost, "that motherfucker is huge!"

"I have come to fight delinquency," said the voicebox. More applause. What the hell was wrong with these people? What the hell was wrong with the world? Why was this funny? Was this punishment? Were they going to watch as it tore off his limbs again? Was this punishment for sinning against the owl under its eternal scrutiny? There was no escaping whatever it was going to be that happened. He hoped whatever it was that it would be quick and it wouldn't hurt much. Usually things didn't feel quick and they did hurt a lot, no more matter how fast he recovered from it.

"John," shouted the Colonel, "stand up. Accept your award."

John stood up and walked up to the creature. He squeaked out a "thank you" as he grabbed the trophy.

"I have come to fight delinquency," said the patriotic ogre.

John scrambled to his seat, left the trophy there, then tried to find himself some place in Bohemian Grove that he might be alone, or as alone as one could be under the watchful eyes of a gigantic owl. He was finding congressmen, debutantes,

Beyonce, grey aliens and high ranking intelligence officers everywhere he tried to slip away. He knew he could not ask for privacy here or ask The Colonel to leave early, so he wandered, panicked up and down the water spitting lawn trying to get as much space as he could between him and the giant.

\*\*\*

"If you're looking for some perspective," said the man covered in cuts and piercings, "then you might want to talk to the Devil."

"Umm…thank you," John forced out.

The guy laughed.

"Oh, no, I bet you think I'm totally crazy. See, The Devil's over there."

The man covered in cuts and piercings pointed at a slight and tiny gentleman clad in a black turtleneck, black pants and a beret. The tiny, slight gentleman was sipping an espresso. From his knowledge of popular culture and movies, John recognized him as a Beatnik. John did not really know what a Beatnik was, only that they used stupid slang and recited incomprehensible poems in coffee houses.

"Oh," said John, "thanks."

"Any time, broheim," said the slashed up man.

John walked away from this guy. He had encountered the Devil in various guises before but had never had a chance to ask him about what was going on.

"You seem troubled," said the mysterious Beatnik.

"Is it true?" asked John.

"Regardless of what your question is the answer that it it cannot be known. Truth is elusive like the unicorn and the unicorn grows rare for it is sick. It is in the throes of taking in our toxins and when our toxins are all in then the unicorn is all out and we are all out of unicorns."

The Beatnik sipped his espresso. That was the sort of answer John expected from the Devil.

"Oh."

The beatnik heaved a heavy heavy sigh.

"You're not especially bright, are you, John?"

John thought about this. He did not excel in school. He was not fond of most books. His music was chosen based upon how loud and angry it was. He seldom watched films with subtitles. He had no desire to travel because he traveled frequently enough. Until recently, he did not think to examine his life or question its purpose. For all of John's faults, he did not have any delusions or pretensions about being exceptional. He knew that many of those around him were of subpar intellect but this was not the same as being sure that he was especially bright.

"No, sir," John replied.

"I am glad that we could get that out of the way," said the beatnik, "it can be hard to communicate with idiots when they think you're talking down to them. Most people are so irredeemably stupid that it's impossible to talk down to them. I'm glad you don't think you're above that."

"I don't think I'm above much of anything."

The beatnik finished his espresso and took two glasses of champagne off a waiter's tray. John had not seen any waiters around this particular neck of the grove before this man finished his drink. John decided not to ask about that. He had earned some respect for this man by being honest about his shortcomings and did not wish to have it taken away by overthinking the situation.

"That attitude will get you far in life. It's getting rarer and rarer these days to find someone who admits he knows nothing. There are people proud to know nothing but their pride indicates that they're better off for knowing nothing and therefore by extension that they know something that those who know things do not. And that is a problem. You can't teach someone who's proud to know nothing. Education requires that someone humble themselves and be receptive to new possibilities. Are you humble, John?"

John shrugged. The beatnik handed him one of the two glasses of champagne.

"You ever drink champagne, John?"

"No, sir."

John had not been given permission to drink tonight by The Colonel. The Colonel would probably have several strong opinions about why he wouldn't want John drinking. Could a bulletproof teen even get drunk? He wasn't sure of this as he did not talk much to the other Crisis boys, who all had the quiet bearing of children homeschooled in a religious tradition. This was not especially far from the truth. He held the glass, uncertain of what to do with it.

"I think you should drink it. That man told you I'm the Devil and if you're looking to get answers from the Devil, you should at least be willing to get yourself drunk at a party, don't you think?"

"I don't really know, sir."

"There's that attitude again, it'll get you far. Or it will ruin you. That, as always is up to you."

John hesitantly took a sip. He looked around for eyes upon him, The Colonel, the owl, but he found none. The feeling of eternal scrutiny was gone, now replaced by one of utter isolation. He took a second sip and waited to see if the beatnik, the Devil's expression changed to one of approval or disapproval, of curiosity or delight. It did not. He took a third sip. It tasted good. It made him feel light and airy and free. He drained the glass and almost as soon as he did, a waiter appeared beside the enigmatic beatnik holding a tray. The beatnik reached for one and handed it to John. John drank again. He felt at ease, if that's what ease felt like. It was obviously not common for John to feel at ease.

"Do you like it?" asked the beatnik.

"Yes, sir," John replied.

"Good. I want you to be comfortable. You have a question to ask and I want you to be able to ask it. I know what it is but I won't answer it if you don't say it. That's just how it works."

John finished the second glass of champagne. A third was quickly in his hand. His invincible body felt weak, like it did in the grip of the starspangled ogre. But his head was getting lighter and the grove and the beatnik were getting much less scary.

"I guess I want to know why all this happens and why I have to get shot all the time. It doesn't feel right. Most kids don't have to go through this and I can't tell what I do it for. Everything feels senseless and weird. Nobody explains anything."

The beatnik nodded.

"And you think I'll be the one to explain. Why do you think that, John?"

"Because you're the Devil and you make all this happen."

The beatnik laughed. It cut into John's buzz hard.

"I don't make everything happen. It's more complicated than that. I don't feel too inclined to explain. But I am glad you asked. I will tell you, John, that nobody wants to be obsolete. The last man selling buggies when the Model Ts rolled off the line felt one of the worst feelings a man can feel. Obsolescence is worse than death. Some people will do anything to avoid it. You know what the difference is between history and trauma?"

John thought about it. He didn't think very hard. He wanted the answer.

"History has happened. Trauma is happening. We have

inverted the two because that's what winners do, they change the game to make sure they never lose again. History is gone, you get trauma instead."

John remembered the bullets he'd taken, the limbs ripped from the sockets, the bodies mangled by the bomb. He thought of all the blood and consequence and the trophy that meant nothing presented to him by a monster. He reached out and found another glass of champagne in his hand and drank it one gulp. The devil was snickering. The man covered in cuts was back and snickering.

"That's it? That's all you can say to me? I've been killed so many times. Why?"

The beatnik shrugged.

"It's not my place to say. Clarity is for each man to find. It is no man's right, no man's possession. I hope that gives you no consolation at all and you get wasted and you fuck up your life."

The Devil would not have been much more informative. The Devil had no more need to give him the truth than did the beatnik. The beatnik was not the Devil. The beatnik was actually an avatar of the Elder God Nyarlathotep. This would not have made John feel any better and for many the difference between the two was almost completely academic. The Devil had not been a PA on the set for the moonlanding and didn't offer Robert Johnson the ability to play the blues. Nyarlathotep had never spoken to Richard Ramirez. A koala is not a kind of bear and never will be. John wobbled away unaware of this. The King of the Dreamlands and ageless patron of flimflam had done his work well.

John grabbed another champagne off the tray, then returned to the slurpee station. Mostly, John just drank slurpees so tonight was very jarring. He hyperventilated as the creamy, fruity swirls filled his cup. He didn't hope to sober up but it was nice to drink something that wasn't champagne and that felt right to him. He concentrated on draining it, suddenly having a feeling that someone was close and that they were watching and waiting. Eventually, he gave in though and looked up.

Kas'sen was standing there, a coy smile on her lightly veiled face.

"You doing okay, John?"

"You said you'd make me an offer," said John, "make me the offer."

She nodded and removed her hat, revealing a forehead with a quivering blue vagina in the center of it. There was light behind it, there was something infinite. He turned it down and she expected, and he fled, screaming. The night became a blur from there.

Dancing with rich girls with nothing to say. Ghostly pale dresses blending together with the ghostly girls inside them. Black judgmental eyes of grey aliens. Laughing reptiles. The owl's brutal scrutiny. The Colonel yelling into the back seat of the limo. The Colonel laughing, almost proud that it happened. Cruel sunlight dragging him from bed.

*** 

John wore sunglasses as he struggled down the hallway of the high school. This place was a toilet before. During John's hangover, it was a rest stop toilet on Labor Day weekend. Grim, hateful faces glowered at him and shoved him out of the way for the egregious crime of trying to get to his locker. Usually, one could expect a certain clique to be more likely to shove you around and treat them like shit. For example, hippies and metalheads might have animosity, religious kids and Goths, jocks and nerds. Usually, this would be the case. But John was not one who had that luxury.

"Move it, fag," said the hippies.

"Move it, fag," said the metalheads.

"Move it, fag," said the religious kids.

"Move it, fag," said the Goths.

"Move it, fag," said the jocks.

"Move it, fag," said the nerds.

"Move it, fag," said the president of the GSA.

One consensus seemed to bring these students together: that consensus was that John was a fag and that he was to be judged for it. They did not mean that he was a homosexual and that his homosexuality made him less human or acceptable. What John was was a fag. This meant he was weak, he was either of loose moral fiber or too square, his taste in music was either mainstream or not sufficiently mainstream. For some reason, John sucked. He did not know why. In his annoyance, he found himself grateful that all of these kids were about to be murdered.

He tried to listen in Science class. He flipped through his textbook wondering where the stuff was on the first meetings with the Greys, the cancer cure, nanoexplosives, Frankenstein labs and chemtrails. There was nothing in there about any of that stuff. These books were stupid. These kids were stupid. He tried to avoid imagining the bloodied crash test dummies that would be left behind after one of them went postal. It got really difficult. Nope. The bullets were already in their heads. They were already slumped unceremoniously against the wall, holes drilled in their heads and chests, disregarded as the murderer moved on until his luck or will to live ran out.

John raised his hand.

"There's nothing in this book about Chemtrails."

The kids laughed. The teacher laughed. Bloodstained puppets with holes in their heads braying at him incoherently, blissfully unaware that death was coming for them in the form of some terrible child with a gun. Assholes. They wouldn't believe him if he told them. Even if he said that somebody in this school was a coldblooded killer and that he knew what was happening but was planted by a conspiracy to sew the seeds of doubt. Even if he told them, they wouldn't believe. They didn't even know about Chemtrails. How did they call this science? At least he didn't have to care. They weren't long for this world after all.

A kid in a Dragonforce t-shirt turned around. John blinked, did his best to not see chunks of his face missing.

"Why are you so weird? What planet are you from?"

There were rumors that Crisis boys had bits of Grey DNA in them or that they were what the Greys had experimented to create. If he was in fact the genetic destiny of man as imagined by space aliens, it would explain his feelings of otherness as something beyond being a mostly homeschooled teenager. But he couldn't answer the question this way. There was no good answer for this kid. Fortunately, this boy was going to die soon. He took the laughter. He slinked into his chair. He closed his eyes to make the corpsefaces go away. He failed to do so, opened his eyes again and reminded himself that he probably didn't give a shit. These weren't good people. Nobody was a good person.

As the lunchbell rang and he slinked into the hall, he remembered that it was not Nobody but rather Almost Nobody that was a good person. Thus far in life, he'd encountered Elsepeth Starlite and she was a good person. A good person that he had betrayed by drunkenly dancing with the bored and dead-eyed daughters and the sometimes lively excitable daughters and the magical nymphlike daughters of the aristocrats and the masterminds and the sorcerers that made America great. He had pressed the close and maybe one had kissed him and maybe two kissed or maybe several had kissed him during the part of the night that faded by dawn. And he had betrayed his girl though she didn't know she was his girl and the reason that she didn't know this was because she wasn't. He considered apologizing though to apologize would be awful presumptuous and completely wrong.

"I like the shades," said Elsie. She liked the shades. Cool. What did that mean? Did that mean that she thought he had good taste? Was she saying "I like you?" but making it soft and noncommittal through deflection? What did she mean that she liked the shades? Was it simply a way of starting conversation? Did she want to hear a story about why he had chosen to wear them? That would make some sense. This was hard. People never say what they mean.

"Thank you."

It was inoffensive. It was direct. It expressed gratitude. It was a good choice. At least he thought so. Maybe there was something better he could have come up with. Probably. He had fucked up. Thank you was an awful reply. She thought he was an idiot. He had lost his shot. He was going to have to spend his life not knowing what that lipgloss tasted like or what it felt like to dance with her like he had danced with a certain number of those girls.

"Are you high right now?"

He shook his head. Maybe he should have lied and said he was high. Nobody here seemed to think he was cool and Elsie seemed to appreciate the fact that he was an outcast. Outcasts did drugs. The devil was a beatnik after all. He'd fucked up again. He'd like to stop fucking up but he did not see that happening any time soon. He tried to save himself.

"No. I got drunk last night at a party."

Elsie's eyes widened.

"Wow, shit, are you okay? I never saw you as the kind of guy who did stuff like that. I don't know you super well but that doesn't seem like you."

Again, he attempted to salvage himself.

"Well, I'm pretty complicated in a lot of ways. I've got

a lot going on."

Elsie was every bit as surprised he said it as he was. This was not a thing that people were supposed to say about themselves. This was just a stupid thing to say altogether . It was clear that Elsie was not sure if he was trying to pick her up or not. It was even clearer that if he had been trying to pick her up with that line, the best outcome would be that she would disregard him trying to pick her up. The worst would be derisive laughter, a Facebook post and walking away forever. The actual result was, like most results of anything, somewhere in the middle. She did not roll her eyes and never speak to him again. On the other hand, she also did not ask to be regaled with stories about his edginess.

"Yeah, that must be tough."

"Yeah, it's tough."

A tower of silence rose from the ground, splitting the Earth on which the conversation happened. Elsie's face said she wanted to gnaw an arm off to escape this boy. John thought her earlobes looked soft. It would be great to have one in his mouth. If that was a thing people did. It might not be a thing people did. He liked being near her and maybe they didn't need to speak. Maybe they were connecting. Yeah, that's what was happening. It wasn't. The silence was not comfortable silence. It was the sound of everything they knew they had in common and the sound of everything he could tell his friends about Elsie and also the names of all of John's friends, including Elsie. There was a hole in Elsie's head and he wanted it gone. He blinked because he wanted it gonebut opened his eyes and found it wasn't gone.

"You okay?"

John nodded. The bullethole was oozing. The bullethole wasn't there but it would be there. It was plain as the cunt on Kas'sen's forehead and every bit as open. Elsie was going to die.

"Yeah, I'm getting tired of these kids calling me fag.

They're such assholes."

"Well, of course they're assholes, they're teenagers. They won't be like this forever."

It hadn't occurred to John that they wouldn't be like this forever. There could come a time when they didn't call him fag and shove him around. There could come a time when they were older and better people and maybe they wouldn't let the world stay awful when they could do something about it. There were people who did something about it, something more than standing there and taking bullets. He didn't like standing there taking bullets and that was all the kids here had to look forward to.

"Maybe they won't."

The bell rang and the two went their separate ways. He wished he could tell her that she should enjoy wherever she was going because she didn't have long to live but it would never come to anything. Warning these kids didn't matter. He'd have to do something to stop this. Elsie Starlite didn't deserve to die and if these kids weren't going to be like they were forever, then they too did not deserve to die. He made his way into the computer lab instead and sat down at a computer.

He would need to find a person who believed him. He would need to find someone who had figured out enough of the conspiracy that when he explained it, they could take action together and shut this down before anyone got hurt. He searched through Sandy Hook videos and watched the denialists and while some cruel talking heads did agree that this was done to take away people's guns, they did not quite have it. They hadn't spotted him. The ones who believed that Sandy Hook hadn't happened thought Bowling Green had. The ones who believed in Bowling Green did not think the Dairy Queen was real. The ones who believed in the Dairy Queen did not believe that Sandy Hook was faked. There were too many agendas competing with one another to isolate one person that saw him and…then there was someone.

Rudy Kazanian slept on Ambien and six beers only because his body required it. His gun was under his pillow though he was sure that if someone was coming that bullets wouldn't do much of anything. Disembowelers. Martian disintegrators, robotic claws made for vivisection. They menaced him with these in his drug fueled dreams as the scarred unicorn on the unicycle looked on, tearing up. There would be no escape. They had his scent and they would use it to follow him anywhere. He might need to burn his laptop and buy a fake ID and go on the road. He couldn't let them get to his mother. They would cut her open and they would fill her with something inhuman. He watched them do this, saw the sexless square infant with blurred genitals slough out of her.

He woke up screaming and picked up his gun, feeling that somehow something was trying to get to him and invade his life. Something was coming and it was going to ruin everything and put him in mortal danger. He looked out through the blinds, expecting to find MIBs patrolling outside. He saw none which did not mean that there were none out there. They were out there. He jumped at shadows, at tiny noises that suddenly thundered. Something was terribly wrong.

He sat down at his computer, wondering if his inbox had been filled with threatening messages or keystroke monitors had been installed and who or what was watching him through his webcam. He had to check for signs and maybe he could figure out how to slip away from them or a means of apologizing for meeting their scrutiny. There was an email, ominous, possibly one of theirs. The subject line was "help me". Fuck. He opened it. At best, it was a virus.

"Rudy-

I believe you. I can't explain until we meet in person. Somehow we're in the same town right now. This is fate. Something bad is going to happen and I need your help. You're the only one who believes in this. You're right about everything. Thank God I've found you. I need your help- J"

He perused the email, nauseous, ready to cry, twitching and afraid. They were gonna kill his mother. This was a sign.

"Please don't contact me. I'm not who you think I am."

"I've read your threads. I know you're the one who can help me. People are going to die- J"

"Never contact me again."

"I need your help."

BLOCK

A sound boomed through the house, an apocalyptic noise, the last noise he wanted to hear. Gun in hand, he went to the door, prepared to put one in the head of an androgynous cybernetic monster of some kind. A teenage kid in sunglasses and a hat was standing there.

"Your mom is in the phonebook. I have to talk to you."

# THREE MONTHS
# EARLIER

"Hey you guys, I was thinkin'," said Kyle Jenson, "about how much Class of 2018 rules."

Kyle Fontaine put his hand on his chin.

"Yeah, you know, Class of 2017, I hung out with some of those guys and they used to say how much they ruled. But that's not nearly as much as we do. I think Class of 2018 is just better."

"Yeah," said Kyle Chen, "Everybody seems so sure that their graduating class is gonna have the most epic Summer ever. But how do you know that? Like REALLY know that?"

Kyle Chen passed the bowl back to Kyle Jenson.

"I guess you don't. I guess it's like a matter of faith that you have the best graduating class in history and your class is the class that rules."

Kyle Fontaine raised his arms as if to disperse a nonexistent ruckus. There was no ruckus and it would not have been dispersed if there was one. The other two Kyles were immediately respectful. There was no need to disperse this hypothetical ruckus.

"What if every graduating class was great? There has to have been a reason where they thought that their graduating class was the best one. Maybe their class doesn't have to be any less great for our class to be great. We don't need to compete with past classes for greatness. Our greatness and their greatness are distinctive from one another. Class of 2018 doesn't have to be the greatest class. We're great in our own right."

The Kyles thought about Kyle Fontaine's words.

Kyle Fontaine was frequently the calm, cool head that counterbalanced Kyle Jenson's more forceful incendiary ways. He had had many stoned and introspective conversations with Kyle Chen and had settled Jenson's temper and tempered his raw enthusiasm. Kyle Fontaine might well have had a point. There was a reason he had been elected Vice President of the student council.

"You know, Kyle, you do make a good point. We don't need to diminish the accomplishments of others to be the best graduating class ever. My opinion is however rooted in the quality of my classmates and the loyalty of my friends. Sure, there will be a guy like you in the Junior class, in fact, I see a little bit of Kyle Fontaine in Quentin Yost. That kid's gonna do good things."

Kyle Chen gave a thumbs up.

"Love the Yost. Ran cross country with that kid. He's fast but you know what? He's humble and that's gonna let him get faster. "

"Agreed," said Fontaine, "Quentin Yost is going places. He could be prom king next year. But I can see you're working up to something."

"I am. Quentin Yost is great but you're Kyle Fontaine. He's Kyle Chen. We have Chucky Baxter, Dave Hernandez, Johnny Ya Ya, P Dog, we've got the coolest class. Mr. Weber was saying how much he'd miss us . You know what? I believe him. We set up that charity carwash, we got the money for the new basketball hoop, we took home a Silver Bowl at College Bowl regionals. We were a great class. Class of 2018 rules and maybe other classes rule too but we should be proud of ourselves and we should act as if Class of 2018 was the best damn class that school ever saw."

"Amen to that," said Kyle Chen.

"Fair point, my friend," said Kyle Fontaine.

The three boys sat together outside of the 7-11, now

enjoying their consensus regarding the greatness of the class of 2018. This soon became a less than exciting way to spend their evening. They had that just graduated and felt aimless, intimidated and unsure of what the vast, dark world presented to them. The awesomeness of the class of 2018 was for this reason moot and not enough to support and protect them on its own. They needed something else, something to help them fight the encroaching dark and cold of adulthood.

"I think we need to do something awesome," said Kyle Jenson, "we know how awesome our class is but we need to do something to get that feeling back."

"Yeah," said Kyle Fontaine, "I agree. This conversation leaves me feeling empty and afraid. Maybe adulthood isn't such a big deal. Almost everyone's an adult. We need to feel like awesome adults or like we're enjoying the last days of our youth. Otherwise, we could just sit here talking about the greatness of our graduating class forever."

Kyle Chen cashed the bowl.

"Agreed. Maybe we need to go get our girlfriends and take them somewhere fun."

"Do you mean like Six Flags? It's been a long time since we went to Six Flags. I could get behind that," said Kyle Fontaine.

"No," said Kyle Jenson, "we need to take them up to Makeout Point. That way we could make out with them and we could drink some beers stolen from my brother's fridge."

Makeout Point had at one time been a very popular makeout spot. It hadn't been called anything at all before it was Makeout Point but then a bunch of teenagers started making out there. This was pretty good for everyone. Teenagers would always need a place to make out. It was good to have an easy, well known place. Before, these teenagers would often get lost trying to find makeout spots. When Makeout Point became popular, this problem faded. There were, however, new problems like a great concentration of teenagers in the same place making out and having sex in their cars. This problem was not all that bad compared to the bigger problems that eventually arose, causing Makeout Point to now be very unpopular as a makeout spot. This did not stop the Kyles, who were high on both marijuana and the coolness of their graduating class.

Kyle Fontaine's girlfriend, Becky Sorriano was not yet high on marijuana or school spirit, though she had served her class well as treasurer and had organized many pep events. It was not that she had no school pride left, it was that it was a measured and reflective pride tempered by realistic expectations and knowledge that this time in her life was fleeting and while the friendships she had made along the way were always to be cherished, this would not be the be-all and end-all of her life. Becky was levelheaded like her boyfriend was and also conscious of her safety.

"We should not go up to Makeout Point. That's where that deranged lunatic with a hookhand killed all those teenagers making out in their car. Sure, the police caught him and gunned him down but there was that copycat taking revenge because some kids backing out of Makeout Point had run down his wife with their car and he thought murdering them under the guise of the hookhand killer would be the perfect crime. You remember that?"

Kyle thought back. Makeout Point's reputation for danger did make it a sexier place but that reputation for danger had not been unfounded. Megan definitely had a point.

"I would say that the place is no longer dangerous but there was the time the copycat escaped and started killing teenagers making out in their cars. He was gunned down by police but they didn't ever find the body. It's probably better that we not take this risk. Thank you, darling, I let my libido get in the way of common sense and I could compromised all our safety with this decision."

Becky stood on her toes and kissed her boyfriend.

"It's okay, Kyle, everybody makes mistakes. If we want a safe, fun weekend we should go to my uncle's cabin in the woods. It's nice and peaceful and quiet. Just imagine, being so far away from town that your cellphone won't even get reception!"

"I love you, Becky. Let's call the others."

At that, Kyle and Becky met up with the others. Kyle Chen had brought his girlfriend Becky Romano. They had been dating since freshman year and had won cutest couple in the yearbook. Becky Romano was more impetuous than her friend Becky Sorriano, a Yang to the quiet and studious Yin of her friend. Their friendship was closer to that of Kyle Fontaine and Kyle Jenson, though Becky Romano's love of fun and freedom rubbed off on Kyle Chen and helped him get out of his shell. Kyle Jenson's girlfriend Becky Patel was an unlikely match. She was into videogames and anime and was a little more sexually precocious than he'd been. She had surprised him by pursuing him and they'd had great times together and he even joined her Saturday D and D game, gleefully battling monsters as a Dragonborn Ranger.

It was a two hour drive toward dark, twisting woods, woods that breathed out the final scream of those who had died in them, woods that bled when the moon was right, woods where wolves grew lean and thin, knowing there were worse things out there than they. Makeout Point was a terrible place, plagued by hook killings. Compared to the area in which the cabin was situated, it was calm, safe and tranquil. There was something big in those woods, something driven only by rage, lust and confusion, moreso even than the teenagers who had come there to raid the liquor cabinet and party.

After a round of truth or dare, the very bold Becky Romano convinced her boyfriend that they should slip off and go skinnydipping. Kyle had never been skinnydipping and felt that these grim, twisting, shadowy woods would not be the place to do so, and the pond looked ominous. It was clear and quiet and still and Becky Romano looked as lovely as she'd ever looked under the fecundity of the full moon. Her smile was big, impish and impossible to say no to, even as fear crept up on him. It could have just been the weed he'd smoked. Kyle had smoked a lot of it. As Becky shook her shorts down her tanned, juicy thighs, enough of his qualms disappeared that he was resolved to be part of this obviously huge mistake.

"Well?" Becky tossed her hair seductively as she ran out toward the pond.

Kyle needed to learn to relax. He needed to learn to get out of his own head. He'd smoked weed to do that but it didn't always work as well as he wanted it to. For the rest, he had Becky. They were going to separate schools and it scared him. He wanted to ask her to marry him but that wasn't going to happen. He would lose touch with her and she would take the joy and courage she had brought him and she would bring it to somebody else. Right now, though, he loved her and she was in the moonlight naked and things were right with the world. It shouldn't have mattered how much time he'd have with her, he had tonight. Kyle took his shirt off, then began to unbutton his shorts.

The wooden spear did its work quickly. It was a brutal weapon but it barely gave him time to feel any pain. It ground down and squished up the organs it encountered, it came out the other side and poured out black, thick, maroon and when it was withdrawn, a lump of intestine. He was already dead the second time the spear entered him but that didn't stop the thing that held it. It wanted to cause damage. It wanted to hurt those who intruded in its territory and those who wanted to feel joy and kinship and touch that it had never known. It continued. Then, when it felt like it was done, it leapt into the water.

Becky Romano had thought the splash she felt was awfully big for Kyle and soon realized something bigger was swimming after her. Becky was a good swimmer, fast and had a couple of trophies for her accomplishments on the swimteam. That could have been impressive if she were trying to outswim something that didn't limbs twice the size of hers, something that dove into this pond to fish from it and find the nourishment that kept its grotesque body going past even death. She stood no chance. It got its arms around her waist and squeezed. Ribs cracked, squished. Bone shrapnel cut into her. Spine divided in two. Sensation ended before it brought her to the shore and lay her down there.

Sensation ended as it had for Kyle but she wasn't dead, not yet. She couldn't feel as it drove a wartridden, gooey, dirtcaked unwashed cock into her and again pressed its massive body against her shattered, barely living form. She didn't survive long before getting squashed completely and bleeding to death but she survived far too long. Like with Kyle, that was no deterrent, it tore apart inside and out , trying hard to attain an orgasm it couldn't possibly get and mangling the broken toy it used because it couldn't do that. Becky's genitals looked like an exploded lasagna by the time it grew frustrated and stopped using her. It dismounted, dragging out its gorecaked penis and then picked up its spear with Kyle still attached.

Upstairs in the cabin, blissfully unaware of the thing from the primeval dark that was coming for them, an ecstatic Becky Sorriano bounced hard on the hardness of an excited Kyle Fontaine. Kyle Fontaine could now understand Kyle Jenson's excitement at the world ahead of them and the pleasures of being young and possessing infinite potential. Becky's firm tits shook as she took in his passion and shit, life was great. Kyle Fontaine would live forever if he could, if life was like this. Class of 2018 ruled. Megan Sorriano ruled. Kyle Fontaine ruled. Megan Sorriano's uncle's cabin in the perfectly safe and pristine woods ruled.

Then suddenly Becky Sorriano went still, hers ears perked up.

"Did you hear that?" she asked.

There had been a knocking on the door, gradually getting harder and harder. It was the sound of the thing beating on the door with Kyle Chen , who was still stuck on the end of its spear. It didn't take many knocks as there was a lot of force behind it. Becky Sorriano was right to fear the noise as it was three knocks with the body before the door went off its hinge and crashed down. It was loud enough that everyone in the cabin could hear it, even Kyle Fontaine but Kyle Fontaine had his girlfriend on top of him and he was high as a kite and drunk and the class of 2018 ruled. Instead of doing something, they went still as rabbits.

Instead of responding to the steps thudding up the stairs, they were still as rabbits, ears perked and uncertain of what to do. If her cellphone had reception, she could have called the police. If her boyfriend had brought his gun, he could have loaded it and gotten ready to put one square in the face of the whatever-the-fuck was coming. He had not brought his gun. One good guy with a gun could hypothetically have prevented this impending loss of life. Of course, that was implying that bad guy was something that was not 8 feet and 475 pounds of perversity,disfigurement and raw hate.

The door fell off its hinge. Becky did not scrambled off her boyfriend, even as he was softening inside her. Becky did not flee. Becky got a spear through the shoulder, penetrating all the way down into the body of Kyle Fontaine. In their last moment, they were pinned together, turned into a pulpy, bloody art installation by the giant that had forced its way into the house and the room as if the room were as vulnerable as the corpse of Becky Romano. It worked the spear a bit to make their insides squish together, a bleeding paste that cohesed their disparate bodies.

Kyle Jenson, man of action had located a hatchet. Becky Patel had been told to get into the damn car. Becky did not. Becky stayed with him, trembling, knowing something was in the house and it was coming, hearing the final piercing deathshrieks of the now dead Kyle Fontaine and Becky Sorriano. They hid around the corner of the kitchen door, locked in an embrace. It thundered down the stairs, covered in gore, naked, erect and filthy, a mass of boils and ingrown hair and mud and moss, giant wild man of the woods. Kyle appraised the situation honestly, finding the Kyle Fontaine inside himself. The Kyle Fontaine who said they were fucked and the Kyle Jenson who loved Becky Patel like life itself became one being, one who was going down defending his girlfriend.

Kyle Jenson lunged with the hatchet and found the monster's kidney. And Kyle plunged it in there, striking hard, again and again and again and again. The creature did scream out, the creature's skin was penetrable, the creature did ooze bile and piss and shit itself as much as it bled. Kyle was doing it. He was hurting the monster that had clearly gone and killed his best friends and was coming for his girlfriend and him. Class of 2018 ruled. Even monsters shouldn't fuck with the class of 2018. He kept stabbing, knowing that there was no stopping until it hit the floor. It turned its head, glazed over eyes that were too far apart, staring at him seeking some semblance of mercy. Kyle Jenson did not give it. Kyle Jenson found its other kidney and let it stain the floor with more blood and diarrhea, let it back up slow organs filled with fish and, when it got curious, people.

It hit the floor and shook the cabin, now soaked in its excrement, eyes pleading, then closing, giant grotesque hardon going soft and retreating into its bilious and pockmarked and hairy and inhuman form. Its chest rose and then it fell and the monster died there. Becky Patel came out from the kitchen and she hugged him, kissed and they cried as one, more in love than ever.

"I love you, Becky Patel," said Kyle Jenson, "I will love you forever."

"I love you, Kyle. I love you so much. I can't imagine anything that could scare me now. We're together and it's going to be fine."

"I'll miss them but I avenged them. I fixed this and this creature will never hurt anyone again."

Becky nodded.

"I'll go start the car."

They broke their embrace and Becky started for the door. They were going to get out of this godforsaken place, they were going to bring the police up here and break the story and Kyle was going to be a hero. At least, that's what was on Becky's mind. Things hadn't gone as planned before and they weren't going to go as planned again. She tried to warn him as it rose up from the floor, soaked in fluids but no noise came out of her. It was faster than it looked.

It took its two huge hands and it clapped. With the force of the hit and the shockwave, it effortlessly popped Kyle's head, sending blood, brainmatter and tiny shards of skull flying. The man she loved crumpled up and fell into that pile of shit, piss and blood that whatever the fuck that was had just risen up from. But she didn't see it.

She might have never forgiven herself but still she knew Kyle wanted her to run and the moment she saw it rise, she started. She had no delusions that he would defeat it, no delusions that they were going to get away and be happy, no delusions that she would get over this and live a life unhampered by the screaming and the stench and the death of all of her friends. She ran out into the dark to get into the car and drive and find someone who could napalm this motherfucking abomination and scatter its ashes and make sure it never got up again. Standing right outside, a man in a military uniform and two weirdos in black suits seemed ready to grant that wish.

"It's okay," said the military man, "my name is Colonel Thackeray and everything's going to be fine?"

Becky looked up, tears in her eyes. She was reminded of Little Red Ridinghood and the huntsman with his axe who had come to cut the wolf open and maybe the wolf was cut open the souls of all her friends would come floating out and make their way to heaven if there was a heaven.

"Really?" she asked.

"Mhmm," the military man replied and shot her in the head.

One of the Men in Black spoke into its wristwatch.

"No witnesses left alive. We require a cleanup team and two strike teams. One team will likely be eliminated."

"Roger that," came a voice over the watch.

The other MIB turned to the military man.

"Colonel Thackeray, it looks like the creature is unstable. Are you certain it will respond to the implants and electrodes?"

The Colonel nodded.

"The subject has already more than exceeded my expectations. This thing is glorious."

\*\*\*

The next sensation John felt was not an unfamiliar one. It had been the basis of most of John's interactions with people, though of course he wished it hadn't. Rudy Kazanian had been taken by surprise the day after an encounter with the Men in Black. He had been ambushed in his home by a stranger in black sunglasses from the internet who would not leave him alone and knew where he lived. There are some very bad reasons to shoot people in the stomach but this was not one of them. Rudy was a nervous, paranoid loner with a gun who had been disturbed in his place of residence immediately after a traumatic event. John did not like it but he should certainly have understood it and had more compassion than most victims of gutshots. He was nonplussed.

***

"Fuck!" John screamed, clutching his chest, "you shot me? Why did you shoot me? I'm trying to help you!"

Rudy did not feel obligated to answer this question. Rudy instead felt obligated to shoot John in the gut again. John staggered back, held himself up from the frame of the door and glared a hole into Rudy that would have been a match for the one his stomach was currently sporting. There is no getting used to getting shot, even for those who survive it on a regular basis. John was not used to getting shot and never would be. He would also never like it. Rudy could now see that John was glaring at him because the force of the second gunshot knocked John's sunglasses off.

"Stop shooting me!" John shouted.

Rudy was grateful that his neighbors were all gone for the day and those who were not had already grown to understand that Rudy enjoyed loudly playing FPSes. Rudy had started cranking the volume of his games to that of an actual gunshot so that the neighbors would not suspect anything if he needed to discreetly fire off a gunshot. Rudy was very paranoid and very fond of his gun. He considered shooting John a third time but it seemed to do nothing to him but annoy him and on some inspection, he saw just who he had shot.

"Fuck! It's you! What are you doing here? Are you here for my mother?"

John shook his head.

"I don't even know your mother. Why would I be here to see her? No, I came here because you know about me and…"

These words were interrupted once again by a gunshot.

John stumbled back further, fell flat onto the sidewalk, bumped his head badly, and left a bleeding gash. There was already plenty of blood on the doorstep already, so when John attempted to stand up, he slipped on it and then fell, hurting his head again. The world began to get fuzzy, the pain almost made his body shut off for a moment and fall unconscious. He steeled himself through it, trying to concentrate and stay strong. This was getting very difficult.

"Pease no shoo I dizzy."

Rudy holstered the gun. There was a bloody mess on the sidewalk, the doorstep and the lawn and all he had managed to do was to make the home invader dizzy and uncomfortable. He had shot first, the time had now come to ask questions.

"Fuck. Get inside. I don't know what you're doing here but I think you know now that I'm not afraid."

"Tanka." John supplemented the bloody mess with his entire lunch, then pretty much fell face first into Rudy's house. This time, he did pass out from the pain. He witnessed a parade of murders and explosions and the deaths of many of his classmates. This was what usually happened when John closed his eyes, though it was now flooding into the waking world. This time out cold was not restful.

"You made a huge mess. It took me like an hour to clean that up. You're lucky I have neighbors who don't ask why I'm bleaching the doorstep or why they heard three gunshots."

"Sorry," said John sheepishly, "I tried to explain in the email but you blocked me."

Rudy rolled his eyes.

"You know, blocking someone via email is usually a sign

that they want you to leave them alone. I wanted you to leave me alone. Not to show up here, get shot, then throw up on my lawn."

"Again, sorry."

Rudy sat down at his computer, opened up his folder on John and pulled up several photos and some of the stills from the Dairy Queen video. He looked at the photos. He looked at the photos, he looked at John. He'd been pretty sure when the kid's sunglasses fell off and then when he brought him in he'd been more sure. Still, he had to check. There was good reason to doubt that this kid was who he thought he was.

"I don't believe in coincidences," said Rudy, "you know because of you, the Men in Black are up my ass. They visited me the other day."

"I'm sorry," said John, "those guys are really weird. The Colonel works with some of them and they come over for dinner sometimes. They never eat anything but he insists on putting food in front of them."

Rudy massaged his temples.

"I have a lot of questions, you know. I don't really know where to start. Most of the guys on the reddit would kill to have my life lately."

"I'm sorry," said John. John could think of nothing else to say. It hadn't occurred to him the things that he was bringing to Rudy's door. John didn't often think of harm coming to himself because his life was nothing but harm. He had thought of harm coming to Elsie and could not tolerate and of how his classmates had been endangered. He had not thought of the scope of the organization Thackeray worked for and what that meant to those he associated with. Rudy was a stranger and didn't deserve this, even though he was a stranger who had no problem shooting intruders in the stomach three times.

"You took three bullets," said an exasperated Rudy, "and you're fine. Are you one of those things, the Men in Black?"

"No," said John, "I'm a Crisis Boy. We show up at the scenes of shootings and massacres. We get killed. People film us. We're there to make some select individuals think that those things never happened. People like you."

Rudy tried to process this. He'd seen the young man on his couch shot at Sandy Hook and killed in the Marathon bombing. He saw him dismembered at the Dairy Queen. The kid died a lot and he kept coming back to life. He had thought the government had wanted people to think that tragedies that hadn't happened happened. He suspected the liberals were using their Hollywood connections to make fake massacres so they could take his guns. He did not like what the kid on the couch had to say.

"Fuck you! You're an actor, or a robot! You're fake and you're trying to trick everybody to get their sympathy. I don't know why you're here but I don't believe you. Those kids didn't die! Those people didn't get blown up! You faked that shit to deceive all the sheeple out there who believe everything they see and read! Well, I don't!"

John sighed. He sat up on the couch. It took a lot to really annoy a kid who got shot for a living but this guy was managing it quite proficiently.

"I took every one of those bullets. I got exploded by that bomb. I watched people crawling to grab their own arms and legs that they'd lost. I came here because you're the only one who believed I was at all those places. You have this backwards. There's going to be another shooting and I need help stopping it."

"Fuck you. Get out of my house."

John stood up and got off the couch.

"Fine. I'm sorry I wasted your time and that you're a stupid asshole who thinks nobody actually shoots children. Is there anybody else who believes I was at all those places?"

Rudy's head sank.

"No. Everybody thinks I'm an idiot. There are people who believe stuff is faked but none of them believe everything is fake. And you're definitely not gonna convince anyone you're invincible."

Fuck. John paced the room.

"Look, I'm sorry. I keep saying that but I am sorry. I didn't mean for any of this shit to happen to you. I want to save these people's lives."

Rudy snickered.

"You never did before. Look at all of these people that you allowed to get shot and blown up and stabbed with scimitars and torn up by that weird, fucked up giant. Why should I believe you're not an actor and that you're not trying to help those things…"

Rudy stood up, got in John's face. He had it figured it out now and these liberal Hollywood conspirators were going to be the ones who were fucked. All their special effects and smoke and mirrors and money weren't going to hide the truth from Rudy Kazanian, the one man who had been smart enough to see through the soundstaged atrocities of the last two decades.

"They were actors too. I understand. This is all just you fucking with me so that I don't expose you, well, I'm not afraid of you!"

"I'm just trying to get some help stopping a bunch of kids from being shot, this is…"

John stopped midsentence. This guy was possibly both stupid and crazy. This man was of no use to anyone, even himself. He wasn't going to get any assistance unraveling the situation from someone who believed that more or less the entirety of 21st century history was a fraud. He took his leave of Rudy Kazanian, feeling more alone than ever.

# GOTTERDAMMERUNG

Nobody had told anyone that they wanted to see bricks fly through windows. Nobody had said to start throwing things at the cops. They were going to get the riot gear and tear gas and starts spraying rubber bullets into the crowd. There was a melee up front with some Proud Boys, the Proud Boys reluctantly joined by some white supremacist skins who would normally not associate with the likes of them. Joanna had tried to back away from the brawl but the brawl was spilling further back. She had wanted good pictures and for her sign to be read and to see what this was all about. What she hadn't wanted was to watch bodies spilling further back into the protest.

The two sides were getting into it harder, knives vs. sticks vs. pepper spray and fists. She had come out to protest, not to fight and still she found herself bodily shoving a fat asshole in a Spartan uniform off of her and getting a loud "Fuck you, dyke!" for her troubles. She tried to fade into the group behind her but she wasn't moving fast enough and the front line was pulling back. The skins and Proud boys were absolute shit but she wasn't feeling antifa cared much about the people in the crowd. Fifty combatants were covering three thousand civilians and the civilians were gonna get gassed and rounded up as cover for the combatants to flee into.

She had not come out to hear bones crunch right beside her or to feel like any moment a bunch of stupid was going to collapse back into her. She fled backwards under pressure of bodies pressing against her, pushing back to gain some space. She'd have to slip out and catch a bus before arrests started or before something worse did. Worse was coming and she could not in a million years have imagined what it was.

The crowd parted ways as the flagdraped colossus walked forward. The combatants tried to stop swinging at each other but it was approaching and it was approaching fast. A couple of the Proud Boys seemed to recognize it, seemed to have a great deal of dread but a lot less surprise. Joanna hadn't seen it before or hadn't imagined such a thing could exist. She didn't know what it was but she slid out of the way to give it space. She didn't flee further than she needed, though or even as far as she did. She was transfixed.

"Citizens, I am Delinquency Man," came a mechanical voice over a voice box, "I am a hero here to fight delinquency. Do not fear, citizens I am here to help."

It shot out a colossal hand, grabbing a masked antifa member in it by the forehead. The young man tried to squirm free but even with just a palm on the head, the grip was fierce, supernaturally strong. The protester's face and body met the concrete, sending shards of it and a cloud of dust and dirt up. The protester slammed down again, squirmed, struggled. Then the young man stopped struggling, stopped squirming. This wasn't real, it couldn't be real. Nothing could be that strong.

Not just strong, it was quick too, picking up another black masked kid. It extended a powerful knee and brought the protester down on it. The snap could be heard through the entire crowd as could the call of "stand down, citizens! I have come to fight delinquency!"It dropped the body on the ground, discarding it with no regard for its life or sentience. Antifa was trying to flee, the Proud Boys were trying to flee but it began to reach out for the other side, grabbing a buzzcut head and twisting, breaking its neck.

"Delinquents, disperse! Assembly is delinquency! Delinquents, disperse! Assembly is delinquency!"

Phone cameras were out, flashes exploding, crowd doing its best to try and get a view of the giant. The giant stopped and waved as if riding by in a parade, then resumed grabbing a fleeing antifa member and tossing them about ten feet into the crowd by the sidelines. Its muscles were spasming into more waving, spasming into a "thumbs up!" It shook and twitched as if shocked by some unseen force. Joanna joined the crowd, pulling out her phone to film it.

Then it approached her. She was concerned her head too was about to be yanked off or her body slammed into the pavement or tossed into the air. Instead, it took her phone in its giant hand, effortlessly crushing it. The crowd looking on and filming pulled theirs back into their pockets. They pulled back as it surged ahead, grabbing for antifa on the run, tossing, grappling, snapping. Its strides were long, its movements surprisingly graceful and it wanted nothing more than to kill. Switchblades and broken bottles smacked into it, not even tearing the costume.

The red and white blue behemoth shrugged off every hit it took. Joanna was looking for a bus but behind her, a blockade had been set up. Police cars, trucks, guys in riot gear. She was trapped. The crowd was trying to run but they'd been corralled in, trapped inside these barricades with the costumed monstrosity, no phone to call for help. She looked for holes in the fleeing crowd, following them and finding that they too had nowhere to go. The gas and the flashbangs and the bullets were behind them and death itself was ahead. Antifa and Proud Boy alike were being beaten, torn, tossed and choked, tiny and insignificant against the thing. It grabbed and smashed a Proud Boy's stick, shoving the broken weapon into his head.

Joanna had never seen anyone killed before and now she

had seen about a dozen, casually murdered by the huge creature in the flag costume. How long before it stopped knowing the difference between combatant and noncombatant? Did it know in the first place? The fleeing crowd, going back and forth between barricades was getting hard to weave around. There was nowhere to go if she could go somewhere. The crowd surged into her, the crowd knocked her down. She lay on the ground, playing dead, hoping that when the monster was done with its terrible work, it would avoid her. She wondered if the world would know what happened to her.

On Reddit, Rudy Kazanian watched leaked footage that caused stir and debate far greater than the Dairy Queen footage. Creepypasta bullshit was a phrase that got thrown around. Independent horror film. False flag operation. Look at this SJW fag on stilts. Fucking SJWs ruin everything. Cosplay fag. Fake. Look at that motherfucker go. Snowflakes deserve it. He's killing ours too, bro. What do you mean "ours?" FAKE. Bad makeup job. False flag. Staged like Sandy Hook. I'll kill you, you cumguzzling childmolester, Sandy Hook was real! How fucking stupid are you? Staged like Bowling Green. I'll kill you, you kike faggot, Bowling Green was real? Wonder what that Raghead Kazanian has to say about this. Armenians are Christians you dumb fuck. A Raghead is a raghead. Kim Kardashian's Armenian. Her dad's a tranny like the Bowling Green killers. You dumb fuck, Bowling Green was staged! SHUT YOUR MUSLIM MOUTH! I'm going to kill everyone at my school. School shootings aren't real. YOU ASSHOLES, TWENTY KIDS DIED! This is just a viral video for the new Friday the 13th. They canceled that! Your mom canceled that.

It was snapping necks, tossing people around like ragdolls. Beating heads into the pavement. Stabbing Proud Boys with broken sticks. Shrugging off stab after stab after stab. One continuous wave of chaos and pounding and gore.

It said it had come to fight delinquency and that assembly was delinquency. Rudy hated these protesters, these UnAmerican entitled little college pussies but nothing and nobody deserved this. He scanned the crowd over and over in hopes of finding John. John would prove that this didn't happen. John would prove that everyone was still safe from monsters and the world would make sense because it was run by agendas that made sense and the Men in Black were only actors like John. John wasn't there. A girl getting trampled by the crowd was there, bodies on both sides were there. Death was there, dispersing the crowd and killing antifa and Proud Boy and skinhead alike. All that everyone was saying was "it's one of yours" or "it didn't happen." Nobody was owning this, nobody really actually cared about all of these people getting murdered by something they couldn't possibly understand. Nobody cared about the truth.

Rudy's mom came in and put the groceries down in the kitchen, then she rushed to the couch and turned on the tv. She was practically bouncing. Rudy turned away from the computer, grateful that he got a momentary respite from all of this carnage and chaos. This gratitude was shortlived, as any peace and quiet had been for the last few days. Peace and quiet might just have taken their leave forever. It was on the news. He wouldn't in a million years have thought that it would be on the television.

The newsanchor was beaming with pride as the still of the giant in an American flag suit came up behind him.

"We live in dark and uncertain times. It's hard for us to tell who's good, who's bad, even whether or not you can believe what you see on television. Well, it's nice, for a change to see Truth, Justice and the American Way personified. The tower of patriotism you see behind you is Delinquency Man. Our nation's youth may be going astray, choosing to cast their lot with extremist causes. They break windows in their protests and throw molotovs at the police. This courageous has said "no more" to delinquency. The Delinquency Man, who, sources say is over eight feet tall and four hundred pounds of pure, all American muscle is here to help. At a protest in Portland, Oregon violence erupted today."

The news cut to a fight between masked antifa protesters and Proud Boys with sticks. There were screams in the background, the crowd was trying to flee the scene.

"The terrorist organization known as Antifa and the free speech activists known as the Proud Boys of the alt right got in an altercation causing an estimated twelve thousand dollars in property damage. It looked grim for the peaceful protesters and the crowd on the sidelines. People were sure to get injured or killed in this imbroglio of rage. But a glimmer of hope has appeared."

The giant again. It was pushing its way through antifa and the Proud Boys and the crowd was escaping. This wasn't the footage Rudy had seen. This had been heavily cut. The thing that had been killing and battering people left and right was being shown helping the crowd get out of the way of the fighting. It went by in a blink and there was still no sign of John.

"I have come to fight Delinquency," said the creature.

The news cut to a lady with a microphone interviewing the monster.

"Wow, you are quite the specimen, if you don't mind me saying!"

"Thank you, Ma'am. I always ate my vegetables."

The reporter laughed. Rudy's mom laughed. Rudy did not laugh. This was not right. This was getting more and wrong by the second.

"So, can you tell me a bit about yourself?"

"I am Delinquency Man and I love America. I have come to fight delinquency and take back the streets for the innocent and the weak and the small. My strength is my conviction and in my heart is nothing but love for the country and its citizens."

Rudy's mother wiped a tear from her cheek.

"Finally, Rudolph, we get a man in a mask who wants to make things right instead of burning things down!"

Rudy's heart sank.

"Yeah, mom, he's great."

"You could learn something from a man like that, Rudolph."

He was learning something from the Delinquency Man. He watched the newscaster shovel platitudes into the masked mouth of the giant and lies into the waiting ears of the American public. He didn't think the protesters were right about the gays and the trannies and the feminists but they weren't this horror. Rudy Kazanian watched the last of the report, then sat down at his computer.

"John-

Let's meet up. You're right. Something is wrong."

***

A digital Derek splattered heads and heads and heads, gleefully strafing down the modded hallways and taking notes in his head. Becky. Becky. Kyle. Becky. Kyle. Round the corner. Eduardo. Jordan. Kyle. Becky. Kyle. Becky. Fuck, how many of these kids were named Kyle and Becky? Then sirens in the distance. Nigel. Travis. Megan. Megan. Megan. Megan. Lot of Megans too. Dropped the handgun, picked up the assault rifle. Didn't have long and the kill count wasn't great.

Patrick. Grace. That little fag John. Warren. Megan. Megan. Megan. The doors burst open and the cops entered the place. He turned the gun on his head. Not good enough.

98

It was just a game he modded but even in this he wasn't getting the results he needed. Too many of these vermin were still walking around. Too many of these snowflakes and fags and homo jocks. He recorded the kill ratio on the path he'd traced out, then returned to the /r schoolshoot reddit.

"Hey, I'm getting really bad scores. I haven't topped thirty on this thing."

The replies flooded in.

"Nobody tops thirty. Have you looked at the stats on Sandy Hook and UCSB?"

"I'm at fifty. What's wrong with you guys?"

"noobz"

"I'm having the same problem. I've been planning to shoot up my school but I can't get above fifteen."

"Twelve here. This game is hard."

"Of course the game is hard, you expect to just shoot a bunch of kids and walk out without the cops coming? What planet are you from? None of these guys survive, that's the point of the game. Some of you guys should get help."

"You should get help with your cum addiction."

"Yeah, go to Cockaholics Anonymous, they'll help you out"

"You should know. You're the president."

"Your mom's the president."

"Up to 16!"

"w00t!"

"60"

"Liar"

"Screenshot."

"Shooped."

"Fuck you."

"I can't get past 13."

"Obama is a Muslim tranny."

"Bowling Green was real!"

"Dicks out for Harambe!"

"Your mom's dick's out for Harambe."

"I modded this for when the Women's Studies class gets out. So many dead fat dykes."

"I gotta do that. But I'm lazy."

"Here ya go."

"Dude, thanks."

"Obama is a tranny Muslim"

"Your mom is a tranny Muslim"

"Your mom is Obama"

"Your mom is Harambe"

"Any tips?"

"Dude, not funny."

"Yeah, post your dick somewhere else."

"Dicks out for Harambe!"

"Your mom is Harambe!"

"Try starting with the assault rifle, then switching to the pistol. Find a concentrated area and spray. Think about where your jocks and the girls who won't go out with you hang out and then go to town. Study halls are good. Cafeteria if you're really brave. Libraries. If you're gonna go through hallways, use a handgun and find cover."

"Thanks, man."

"Yeah, good tip."

"Here's a good tip."

"NOT COOL."

He tried again. He stayed inconspicuous, then headed into the library. He let loose with the assault rifle, strafing around the room. A couple headshots, a couple hits in the shoulder. A few bullets in the neck. Probably about five fatalities there. Not bad. Five dead, six injured. A lot of them were taking cover under the tables. A lot of cover but a lot of people. The librarian was creeping off. He pulled the handgun, made a clean headshot. Good but conspicuous. He headed out into the hallway, where kids were already trying to get refuge inside of classrooms. Handgun in the hallway.

Jason had called him a queer goth pussy. He shot Jason in the back. Not sure if it was lethal but it was sure as hell worth it. A Kyle. A Megan. A Becky. He was in the groove. Kyle. Megan. Becky. That fag John. Elsie. Too bad. She had nice tits. Becky. Becky. Josh. Josh. Jennifer. Becky. Megan. Becky. Becky. Kyle. Becky. Ethan.Kyle. Shit, he was on a roll. Sirens. Not a bad score so far. This run had potential. There was some controversy on the Reddit over libraries, a hill many schoolshooters ended up dying on but Derek was having a good run. 26. Not bad.

Derek put on Pornhub, jerked off over a job well done.

* * *

Baseball cap. Sunglasses. The best and most effective of all disguises. He sat down at the booth at the Roy Rogers, watching the room. Pygmies. A couple ninjas. A guy in a pug suit. Normal Roy Rogers crowd. He had been told once that Roy Rogers was the one place in America that the NSA never bothered with surveillance on because it was simply too stupid. He wondered if the others here had come to this place for that reason. Rest stops were an intermediary space between not only home and vacation but between light and darkness, between sanity and madness. MIBs were terrified of Roy Rogers, according to the rumors, and not especially fond of Sbarro.

A beehived waitress with a fake mustache approached the table.

"You know you order up front, right?"

"Then why is there wait staff here?"

"You ask too many questions, son."

John examined his watch. Rudy was fifteen minutes late.

101

Maybe he wasn't coming. Standing him up would be a weird way to punish him. Rudy was weird though. Probably also unstable. If that's what he was up to, it wasn't funny. It was scary. He'd seen the news report and how the Thackerays beamed with pride. The Colonel with maybe too much pride. John hadn't thought to ask if he anything to do with the monster because he knew the answer. It had, after all, presented him a trophy.

Rudy arrived a few minutes later.

"Sorry. Traffic."

"Whatever."

"What?"

"I know you were pissed, just admit that you intentionally made me sit here and wait."

"Are you seriously going to be like that? After all the shit you've brought down on me."

"You shot me three times."

"Please, have the people in this restaurant have shot someone."

John looked around. He was probably right. This Roy Rogers was filled with the dregs of society and several people who couldn't even be classified as the dregs of society. John was pretty sure one guy was naked. Regardless, John did not like waiting and he did not like getting shot. Rudy had done both things. He was once again regretting ever getting involved with this guy.

"Well, asshole," said Rudy, "I'm here now and I don't have a gun in my hand so let's talk about this situation."

"Okay, you fat, worthless piece of shit. Agreed. Let's discuss the situation."

"Sure thing, you socially retarded government stooge."

Rudy waited for John to insult him back. John waited to come up with an insult. He decided it wasn't worth it and that they had very important things to do. They had very important things to do from the getgo but the animosity took center stage more than the urgency. There was no other insult this time.

"So, I get dispatched to places when things are about to happen."

Rudy nodded.

"How do they know?"

John shrugged.

"Magic, time travel, I couldn't tell you if I wanted to. They're weird. Somehow they know things and they know that they'll need someone there to be seen getting murdered or blown up or whatever. That person is sometimes someone else but this time it's me. That's why I've been transferred here."

"To the town where I live? That seems awfully convenient. Maybe too convenient."

"I don't know. I don't feel like this has been particularly convenient for me. I feel pretty inconvenienced."

"What if they want to get rid me through you?"

John thought about it. Was there a reason they would want Rudy out of the way? They had wanted somebody to see John and some people saw John and they had wanted this person to reach the conclusion that everywhere John was, whatever seemed to be happening wasn't happening. There had not been many people who had, so Rudy sounded like the person they would be least likely to want to kill.

"I don't know why they'd do that. You're the only one who saw me all those places."

"Exactly."

"But they wanted you to see me there."

"What if they didn't?"

John thought about this. It could have been a complicated setup. It would have been insane though.

"If they didn't want to people to see me, then they

wouldn't put me there to be seen, right?"

Rudy contemplated this. There were a lot of conspiracies and counterconspiracies at work and there could be any number of reasons for John being there. There could be something more complicated at work than either of them could have perceived. There could be something that made no sense at all.

"I guess," said Rudy, "we can figure out that out later. What's important right now is that you go over what you know about the situation."

The waitress approached the table.

"You gonna order something?"

John walked to the counter, ordered a double cheeseburger and a shake then sat back down. Rudy, directly behind him, ordered the same thing though did so cognizant of John's statement that the Men in Black enjoyed milkshakes. It was awfully suspicious that John too enjoyed milkshakes. But why would he say he enjoyed milkshakes? Was he trying to intimidate him? And why were they at this weird rest stop? This rest stop was really weird. And how did a teenage kid make it out to this rest stop without his parents noticing? This was very fishy.

They sat down again.

"How do your parents not know you're here?"

John shrugged.

"The Colonel's off doing stuff. You'd think he'd keep a better watch on me but they don't really care what I'm up to when I'm not doing one of their missions. That's not important though, this is the one place they never bug or spy on. Nobody cares about the Roy Rogers, this one especially."

"Weird."

"I know."

"So, why do you need my help again?"

"I want to stop this shooting?"

Rudy sighed.

"And you didn't want to stop any of the other ones? You stood back and watched a lot of tragedies happen. What makes this different from all of those, huh?"

John did not want to think about all of the times when he felt somewhat compelled to intervene and decided not to. When he thought about this, he thought about himself as complicit in the slaughter of a great many innocents, which he had very good reason to think. Therefore, he had very good reason to not want to think about that. If he was going to work with Rudy, however, he was going to need to come clean.

"Okay, look, there's a girl. Okay? I let all those people die because none of them was a girl I like. I feel like an asshole but that's how it is. It still doesn't matter because we're still preventing a bunch of kids from being killed."

"Fuck you."

"What?"

"I said, fuck you, kid. You let everybody suffer until you meet a girl you like? Fuck you. Where were you for any of those others?"

John could not answer that question.

"I'm a teenager. Weren't you selfish when you were a teenager?"

Rudy thought about it. He kind of felt bad for the kid. Rudy had gone through his entire life without being shot once and this kid had survived it three times in the past two days, all of them at his hand. He too had been selfish and difficult as a teenager even though his mother had called him a prodigy and said that any girl was lucky to have him. This kid was most assuredly not a prodigy at anything but taking large quantities of bullets.

"Okay, so you want to save your school, what's your plan?"

John did not have a plan. John had never been required to have a plan. He had grown up surrounded by people with plans. Perhaps to the point where planning had rubbed off on him. This was an optimistic assumption on John's part. John was a patsy, a stooge and a pawn. He was not equipped for masterminding anything more complicated than sneaking out to a rest stop to tell a guy he met from the internet that they needed to come up with a plan. He did not want Rudy thinking this, so he came up with a plan.

"Well, I don't know who the killer is and I don't know my classmates well enough to determine who it could be. They mostly just shove me into things and call me fag."

"Yeah, sounds fair. I saw you and immediately felt like shooting you."

The food came. They began to eat.

"Well, anyway, because of that, it will be hard for me to figure out who is a potential shooter."

"Agreed," said Rudy, taking a mouthful, "so whatsaplamb?"

John was not proud of his plan.

"Since we don't know which person is the shooter, we need to look up who owns gun and then take their guns away. I'm sure if I explain it's to stop a violent crime, they'll be willing to listen."

"Fuck you!" said Rudy, spitting bits of meat at John, "my gun is how I express myself! Taking people's guns is part of the Gay Agenda!"

"I don't know what the Gay Agenda is but it's the only way. We need to prevent these killings and anyone with a gun is a potential suspect."

Rudy thought about it. His gun was an extension of his masculinity and individualism but surely people would understand that public safety in the wake of a potential disaster was far more important than that. It only stood to reason.

"I don't like it but you've got me convinced," said Rudy, "here's my gun."

"I thought you said you hadn't brought it."
"Nah, I take this thing everywhere."
John put on the concealable holster.
"Okay, good, there's one."

# JOHN AND RUDY TRY TO TAKE EVERYONE'S GUNS

They failed. Nobody could possibly do that.

# JOHN AND RUDY REGROUP
# AT THE ROY ROGERS

John and Rudy regrouped at the Roy Rogers. They had gathered exactly one gun, which belonged to Rudy. John could have been the last survivor of the gunhatingest planet in the solar system, then gotten bombarded with cosmic gun-taking rays and then returned to the Earth with the powers of taking everyone's guns and still he would probably have had had fewer guns than he needed to make sure nobody at the school got ahold of a gun. The number of guns he would have needed to assure this was "All of them". And this was, of course, impossible. John and Rudy were now the two people least happy to be at the Roy Rogers. This was a momentous accomplishment, though they obviously didn't see it that way.

There was once more a waitress approaching the table. The waitress was blue and irresistible and to John, she was familiar. John considered reaching for Rudy's gun. Rudy considered offering the contents of his wallets, the keys to his house and a couple of kidneys to the shapely creature in the leopard skin pillbox hat. Rudy did not know why their table was being waited at a restaurant without waitstaff by a stunning lady with Jacky O headgear and he did not bother to ask questions.

"What'll it be?"

John glared.

"What are you doing here?"

Rudy glared at John.

"Are you always this rude? The lady's just trying to do her job."

John sighed.

"How is it that this is not setting off any red flags? You're the paranoid one. Do you see any other waitresses here? People are ordering at the counter, like they always have. This woman does not belong here. Her name is Kas'sen and she is a space prostitute of some kind."

"Why would a space prostitute be on Earth? They work in space."

The waitress nodded.

"Yup, this one's very sharp."

John moved one hand down toward Rudy's gun.

"Why are you here?"

"To take your order. And you're holding things up, John."

"Double cheeseburger," Rudy declared, "Rare. With a chocolate milkshake."

The waitress jotted it down on her notepad.

"No, really. What are you doing here?"

"John, we both know you're not going to shoot me or anyone. You have an instinctual fear of that device that you're trying to reach for. And I don't blame you. If I were you, that thing would make me sweat and hesitate, increase my heart rate, blood pressure and breathing and be useless for me in a high stakes situation. I'm going to level with you idiots, okay?"

John made no indication that it was okay. He was getting annoyed. Perhaps his ability to resist this woman was similar to his ability to survive a hail of bullets. It was probable that the two were equally poor for one's quality of life. He had seen into Kas'sen's head after his conversation with The Devil and wanted nothing to do with it. He still waited and listened.

"There are two ways this can go. You boys can get your dicks sucked or you can fuck everything up. This is the Gay Agenda you're dealing with. You have no clue what they're capable of."

Rudy leaned in to whisper in John's ear.

"John, I think we should take her offer."

"I respect your honesty," said John, "but I think instead, I'm going to fuck everything up. It seems like the right thing to do."

The blue waitress shrugged.

"Well, I tried. And then I tried again. I don't know why I care about this. Probably because shit's about to get weird."

\*\*\*

Rudy didn't want to shake where he sat. He didn't want to retreat or tell John "I'm out." It was getting difficult to do that. This was not going to get simpler. Even if the shooting was thwarted, what about the people who wanted that to happen? He really wanted that blowjob. She looked like she'd be really good at it and it was a nice offer that John shouldn't have shown so much resentment for. Rudy said nothing. Rudy sat still. He'd always wanted to be something better than a twitchy, angry gamer who lived with his mom. His dad had been all about being manly and honorable up until he put a gun in his mouth. This was Rudy's chance to do that. He wasn't invincible like the kid was but he'd try and act like it. He kept his mouth shut, which was the most heroic thing he could do.

She shook her head and left, leaving John and Rudy to strategize and take in just how ominous her warning had been. The answer to that was VERY. Neither of them knew what the Gay Agenda actually was, how much the Gay Agenda was capable of what the consequences of defying it could be. If Kas'sen was this concerned, those consequences would have to be high. Unless of course they were actually afraid and Kas'sen was being used to prevent them from defeating a very defeatable enemy. Both of them came to this conclusion in their mind and both of them eliminated it. Life was not that fair.

It was John who broke the silence.

"She didn't take our orders to the counter, you know."

"Yeah."

From there, they ordered food and returned to their seat and began to discuss plans.

"Well," said John, "we now know that the Gay Agenda are the ones who planned this and maybe the ones The Colonel and the Men in Black are working for.

\*\*\*

Hathaway and Crenshaw blazed hot lead through mercenary gypsies, a Lewis and Clark of slaughter. The two were close, best buddies ever and they always had each other's back. Behind those backs, before the secret black ops days, there was talk that they were more than friends, jokes about it. Certain fools had tried to joke about to their faces but were soon relieved of not only their misconceptions but several of their fucking teeth. They were brothers in arms and nothing more and this black ops Roma KGB hit squad was about to learn what that brotherhood meant. It meant death. American style.

The gypsies had discovered in the tarot that Hathaway and his elite squadron of former master criminals were coming. They were crafty and wise in the ways of fortune telling and managed an ambush that blew up the team's battle van, rendering its Freedomfinder missiles, its buzzsaw launcher and its rockets useless against the bandana'ed hordes of knifewielding bandit fortune tellers. They had lost Jakob Krantz, Nazi scientist brought over from Project Paperclip, Alessandrlo Bracchetti, disinherited Italian count turned conman, Problems D'artagnan, Black Panther strongman and master asskicker, Aberdeen Harry, Scottish demolitions expert and sociopath and Miss Lenore, circus knifethrower turned safecracker and burglar. They had done many very secret missions and gone on several colorful and fascinating adventures. But they were dead now.

In the heavily wooded mountain pass, covered in burnmarks from having rolled out of a blown up battle van, Thackeray had turned full on berserker, gritting teeth and shrugging off knifewounds from graceful murderers used to the subtle and sensual dance of killing an gifted with their blades. Though he was getting slashed up, he still had ammo in his gun, breath in his lungs and blood in his body. He was going to fight on no matter what. Headshot, gutshot. The colorful band of thugs drove into him but he was a crackshot, cruel and certain of the inferiority of those he fought. As knives dropped, he picked them up, opened guts, then dropped them and though his ammo was running low and he was growing tired, the bodies were hitting the floor and Crenshaw was dropping them just as fast.

Marshall Crenshaw, buzzcut, squarejawed linebacker shouldered angel of Cold War aggression was waste deep in the dead, and there wasn't a mark on him. God was on his side apparently and didn't want one of America's finest and angriest sons brought low by pagans with thick beards, strange accents and some kind of occult mojo that made them master bushwhackers of the highest order. Hathaway had just been killing, just been shooting and slicing and dehumanizing but Crenshaw remembered the mission, even though their comrades were dead they needed to die for something.

"I know some of you pieces of shit speak English, so I'm only gonna ask once," said Crenshaw holding up one of the assassins, an old woman in flowing purple skirts in his powerful hand, "where is Agent Putin? Who are you working for?"

The gypsy merc laughed a wicked laugh.

"Oh, do you want to see who were are working for? That can most certainly be arranged, Americanski."

Crenshaw tightened his hold.

"Is that a threat?"

The gypsy cackled again.

"We do no need to make threats, we have seen the future. You are not long for this world, Americanski."

"You don't know what you're fucking with," he said, kissing her hard to prove that he could, "we're the biggest badasses America has to…"

He didn't see the great black shape, the enormous bat descending from the sky. The tenebrous blur came down hard, pinning him to the ground, then tearing out a big, thick slab of throat-meat. Spray, splurt, squish, then quick as it came it was gone.

Hathaway looked around him. This Agent Putin was resourceful, his Roma underlings far more vicious and driven than he had initially thought. Hathaway cursed himself for underestimating the guy. His team, his brother, they were all gone and he was alone faced by a horde of strange miscreants who had seen him coming with magic. As they descended on him, he kept slashing, kept fighting, even as his body grew weaker. His spirit was willing but the flesh, the flesh was… the world grew black and Trannsylvania faded in favor of only fuzz and darkness and regret and missing his friend.

He awakened to women in white Muslin, pale and etheric as human fog, bodies lithe, impossible and optimal, on the verge of mirage. Their lips were cherry red and they were caressing him, brushing sharp canines against his body, which had been stripped naked. Their skin was cold, their eyes like those of vixens. He was chained down to wall someplace deep and dark and did not know how long he had been out. He wanted answers but he did not want them to stop touching him, cold though their touch might have been.

"Do you speak English?" he asked them.

"Our English is perfect," said one, sliding a tongue up and down his bare chest. He quivered, rattling his chains.

"We are not savages here. We are very well educated and here to make you feel at home?"

This wasn't right. This was weird. He had to still be in Transylvania. Him and his team had gone down at the Borgo Pass and then he'd lost consciousness and was in the dark with the strange, predatory, pale women touching him.

"At home? Where is this?"

"Shh…" said the third. Then, with a hiss, she opened her mouth and moved to take a bite out of his throat.

He could have been eaten. He could have been killed in an instant. But, that wasn't what fate and the master of this house had in store for him. A booming voice echoed through the chamber, causing it and Hathaway's chains to shake.

"STOP! He is not for you!"

They let out cries of grief, moans of frustration, then animal howls as they scurried away at the entrance of a tall figure with salt and pepper hair, the owner of the clear, deep booming voice. Tall, imposing, with sharp, distinguished features a regal bearing and a great black cloak. There was only one person this could not be and it could not possibly be that person. He was having this hallucination as he bled out on the pass, left for dead by Putin's killers. Obviously, it could not be. Hathaway asked anyway.

"Who are you?"

"I am Dracula," the imposing figure said, "welcome to my house."

"What? Why?" Thackeray struggled to gain some semblance of bearing in this dungeon, "How?"

"Major Thackeray, you have been quite a thorn in our sides, you know that?"

"Are you going to kill me?"

Dracula laughed.

"Goodness, no! I do not practice such barbarism upon my guests. None are as hospitable as those who are cannot enter an abode unbidden. No, you shall leave here alive or you shall never leave here. I hope that provides you some succor."

There was nothing Thackeray could have heard right then that would have provided any semblance of comfort or calm. He wished he had been killed on that pass rather than having to see his dearest friend die and every one of the legends at his command blown up in their awesome van. Life could not offer him much now.

"You killed my best friend. You killed my team. I'd rather you just kill me right now, please. Besides, if you don't, I will find a way free from these chains and I will put a stake on your heart, you creepy foreign fruit!"

Dracula stroked Thackeray's face. He stared into his eyes and though Hathaway tried to break his gaze, he could not.

"Oh, my dear Thackeray, you are alive right now because I know for a fact that you would. I am not unfamiliar with your exploits or that you would leave my castle in my flames and my coffins broken and destroyed. My fortune tellers saw that very possibility. I have missed my dear Dr. Van Helsing over time and a worthy foe more than piqued my interest. I would simply let you free to fight again and overcome your grief but my associates, my masters want to offer you something much grander."

"Then why am I chained up?"

"The fortunetellers say that there is a possibility of you refusing and should you refuse, you will be a great danger to their plans, so much so that you our only choice would be to keep you here and to leave you to be the plaything of my wives."

Thackeray forced a smile to seem like he had some control over the situation.

"There are worse fates."

Dracula laughed again.

"You are delightfully droll, Colonel."

"I'm a Major."

"For now. But you could be so much more. You could go from just being a violent marionette dancing into death defying violence over and over again for only the reward of knowing that you stabilize what you believe and you would call The American Way, if only because of your naivete. You have chosen Agent Putin as your foe because you believe this to be a game of chess between America and Russia and that the prize will be the stability and philosophical triumph of a way of life."

Thackeray did think that. There was no reason to think anything else and this vampire creep wasn't going to convince him otherwise.

"I know how you Russkies work. Kill me now, you bastard, I'm not gonna give in to you Commie sons of bitches and your faggotry."

Dracula leaned in close.

"Faggotry, you say? The world is so much more complicated than you think and when you are educated and ready, you will add richness and nuance to it, spice the soup instead of pissing in it."

"Who the fuck do you work for?"

Dracula turned around.

"I don't know if you're ready…"

"Then finish me."

The vampire put his hand on his sharp, noble chin.

"I suppose I'll just say it."

"Yeah?"

"Welcome to The Gay Agenda."

\*\*\*

Twenty seven kills, stonecold cowboy badass deathmachine Derek had a boner that almost couldn't quit. He scrolled through photos of dead cheerleaders from other crime scenes and beat it like an egg, beat it like it owed him money beat it like he beat the preppie scum that polluted the halls with their laughter and their vapid joy and their not one of us and their perky tits and their asses in their tight sweatpants and their laughter into their hands at the mere thought of Derek. They were always laughing into their hands at the mere thought of Derek. But you could see up the skirts of the dead ones, their bleachblonde heads soaked in brain matter and fuck, oh, fuck, they look so fucking good why couldn't they suck his dick instead of all those ignorant jock gorillas who gave nothing to the world and took took took until the day came when they could go out on Daddy's money and not now not now not now no…

He finished, put on some music and lay there in postcoital, postmurder bliss. He smiled at the ceiling and let the contentment wash over him. There had been moments of nagging, moments of hesitation and moments of doubt. There were moments where he thought he would be stopped before he even started. No, that wasn't going to be the way. He could do this. The guys on r/schoolshoot were supportive, they understood and their scores were seldom as good as his without the hacks or the mods. He returned from blessing and turned on his webcam.

"This is for all the people who are fed up. This is for the nice guys who can't get pussy because the quarterback has the girl. This is for people who can't get a job or get into school because affirmative action's taken the jobs from them. This is for the people who just want to play their videogames without liberals censoring them. This is for everyone who loves loud music, being un-PC and imagining a world untouched by so-called progressives. I'm mad and you're all mad. I hope we all take a stand like this , I hope we take things back. We've been bullied for too long but we have brains and guns and skill. We have passion and we will win. Tomorrow, I'm going to kill as many people as I possibly can. Everybody who sees this video and believes me understands that this must happen. The rest of you think I'm just another Pepe. There is no future for me. There is no love, no hope and no "progress", thanks to the progressives and the feminists and the bullies of the world. What I do tomorrow is for all of you."

He posted to schoolshoot and he thanked everyone there, remarking that tomorrow was the day. This would be the last night of his life. Some people would want to eat their favorite meals or call their parents and say they love them. Some people would feel a deep regret about the things they would never do. Those people do not shoot up their high school assuming that they would end up killing themselves. He made all the arrangements to make sure people would know what he was all about before the spree happened. He rewatched Delinquency Man handling all those protesters. At least the world had one hero. Two.

Though conspiracy theorists do have to look far and wide for research materials, Rudy Kazanian was not necessarily a world class hacker or a skilled detective. There were not many occasions in which these deficits and lack of knowledge of the methodologies involved would prove beneficial but sometimes weird things happen. Sometimes forces converge in such a way that laziness and ineptitude become a useful skillset and exactly what the conflict at hand called for. Other conspiracy theorists were not looking to thwart a future schoolshooting that would soon be committed by a Reddit and Youtube savvy individual.

119

Rudy had forgotten about the existence of r/schoolshoot and had also been told that no actual crimes had ever been traced back to schoolshoot. This was, like many things Rudy read, untrue. He didn't have high hopes for r/schoolshoot but r/schoolshoot exceeded his wildest expectations. What Rudy found was Derek. Derek whose scores were at first too low but getting better, Derek ranting on Youtube, Derek saying it was the time to kill and that he thanked everyone who had helped him. Rudy had assumed schoolshoot was bullshit and that these people were all trolling but what he found would shake him.

These people did not have regard for dead children. These people did not care that he was going to walk into his school with a bunch of weapons and blow away everyone that had ever pissed him off. They instead had given him their blessing and told him that they understood and that all of them were ready. They posted memes deriding the future victims, posted gifs of cheerleader heads exploding and long tirades about the girls who wouldn't fuck them and how they were ready to take them down too. He'd seen a lot of callousness from the conspiracy people but had not expected disregard like this for life itself. He felt sick. He watched the video over and over again, hoping at once that the lead was false and that he was dead on and had an opportunity to stop it.

There were names on the schoolshoot thread and on the commentary of the Youtube video that he had seen before on r/conspiracy. He wasn't sure he considered them friends but he'd considered them like him. Was he like them? How much? Rudy Kazanian held his gun in his hand and thought about his father. His father had always said life was unfair but that one had to be an honorable man in spite of it and work hard and take no shit and defend what was yours. His father always said life was unfair, then with a single pull of the trigger, he made it moreso for his son and wife forever.

\*\*\*

Rudy held the gun and began to sob. When this was over, he would either be killed or he would not be needed anymore. Who had he been to think he could contribute anyhow? He was a fat loser who still lived with his mom and hadn't had a girlfriend in seven years. He had a job he hated and nobody he was excited about hanging out with. He was excited about games and tv shows and leaked videos on the internet. He was not excited about people and about events that were happening in his life. There was nothing for Rudy to look forward to. He wasn't that different from Derek and those jeering masses at all. He just wanted to be someone who made people's life better, including his own. He wanted to be the man his father tried to be. Rudy's mother would have nothing when he was gone but she would also be free of her family and free of the face that reminded her of her husband. If he was going to die though , he did owe someone something and he could one last bit of good.

He dialed his phone.

"John, pick up, it's Rudy, I think I got the guy."

At the end, there was silence, loneliness and the hum of nothing going on again. He couldn't help but be reminded of the nothing that waited for him. He texted John.

"Seriously, we need to talk."

Rudy waited and watched the video again. There was no good reason to torture himself with this beyond the sudden and inescapable sensation that he had done something to deserve this. He hadn't been easy to be around and he hadn't felt any inclination to reach out or to make himself better. He was seeing that pay off now, seeing the face of his enemy and a heart not unlike his own. He felt really bad for the kid. This was a boy who had nothing to look forward to to the extent that he could kill everyone he knew and lose nothing and be no less lonely for it. Rudy could kill everyone he knew and he wouldn't be that much more lonely. Fuck. Pick up, you asshole.

"John, I need you to pick up. This isn't just about the thing but I have important news about the thing and I don't know we don't know each other very well but I'm freaked out and I need to talk to someone because this is too fucking much, John. I don't know if I can get through this night. I need to talk to someone."

Rudy was smarter than everyone. Rudy was a rugged individualist who didn't believe everything he read. Rudy shot straighter and played better than his Overwatch team, who were the only voices he heard that didn't belong to his mother or Youtubers. He didn't want to reach out to his Overwatch team. Those guys could go fuck themselves. He wanted to reach out to his Overwatch team but they didn't get it . They wanted to play a game to calm the fuck down. Rudy would not calm the fuck down. Calming down was not in the cards. There was a gun in his hand that wanted to see the inside of his mouth and the bullet wanted to see the top of his head.

"John, you goddamn motherfucking cocksucker, I need someone to talk to right now. You're my best friend and we don't even like each other. I know this guy. I mean I don't know him but I know people who know him and I talked to them like they were regular people and they were like me and fuck, John, my dad killed himself. He shot himself. I'm going to do it, John. I can't take this. I'm sorry. I'm not like you. I'm not unbreakable. Help me. I need you to help me. You son of a bitch! I'm helping you. I decided to do this with you and save those people and you're ignoring my fucking calls. Well, fuck you, John! Fuck you, you fucking freak!"

He returned to the gun to the drawer and cried into his hands. The night would be long and dark and full of terrors for Rudy. He stayed up waiting for a call that did not come and a text that did not come. He stayed up wrestling with a gun left in a drawer and the possibility of no more possibilities that it presented. He dreaded the coming dawn and he dreaded the dreams he would have if he were to go to sleep but he dreaded the morning more because he had made a decision now and the consequences of that decision would be heavy. He envied John not having to deal with that but wouldn't have if he knew what John had gone through.

John was naked in a plexiglass booth being observed by Thackeray and two curvaceous ladies in labcoats that he suspected were not scientists but strippers that had been paid to dress like scientists. The thought was sexist, for these women's voluptuous bodies did not indicate that they were any less proficient in STEM subjects than a man would be. Though this thought was sexist, it was also true. These women observing him were not scientists but rather strippers disguised as scientists. What John was about to go through had literally no scientific merit at all and was already well documented.

"What are we going to do?" John asked, full of concern. There was something terribly fishy about this experiment, even for one of Thackeray's experiments. It was if he was purposely trying to show that this was not a genuine scientific effort and should not be mistaken for one. The only reason this would be would be to promote fear and compliance. That would not be outside of Thackeray's wheelhouse, especially in light of recent events, which John hoped were not a factor in this experiment.

"If we tell you," said one of the stripper doctors, "then it will change the results of the experiment."

That didn't sound right but it was probably best to play along.

"Oh. Yeah, that makes sense."

It didn't. The Colonel hit a button on a remote in his hand and the experiment's nature revealed itself. They came in a cloud, as both burns and pinpricks and heat inside. They filled the both and head to toe, he experienced them and their wrath. The welts, the boils, the puzzling. They struck him on his chest, his nipples, under his armpits, on his eyelids which soon swelled shut, mercifully so he could not see the boils and the mass of pink nonsense his body was turning into. It was healing, it was fighting, it was struggling with the bee venom but not suppressing the pain. The Killer Bee Test. He was being Killer Bee Tested. He wanted to scream out and ask why or if they would stop but his lips were quickly swollen shut by all of the stings.

They were entering his nostrils and stinging inside of there, the welts and boils and stings swelling and thickening and shutting his nasal passage. They were between his thighs, stabbing him in the balls and the scrotum. The pain was such that it stopped being pain or everything that was not pain faded. He had been blown up and dismembered. But this ad known all manner of pain before but this had been chosen, handpicked to exhibit the human body's potential for suffering and to remind John that there were things much worse than death. He would survive this and it might not be the last time he would have to live through it. Suddenly, a woman was sobbing.

"Please, please don't, I promised you confidentiality, please…"

The shot was loud. The scream of the other "scientist" was loud. The next shot was loud, so was the thud against the floor. The Colonel could have silenced his guns but drama was important right now. This needed to be scary.

"What you just heard, queerbait," said The Colonel, "is the sound of the two of us being left all alone. Kas'sen tried to stop you and reason with you. She offered you something planets have fought wars over. You're a teenager though, John, you don't understand opportunities and privileges you only understand how bad you feel, don't you?"

124

John struggled to make a noise. He of course failed.

"Of course I know you can't talk right now. Your lips have been swollen shut. Hell, I bet your asshole's been swollen shut. This is one of the worst things that can happen to you. Not the worst, John. I could make you drown in your own diarrhea. I can cut you for days with knives carved from your own bones. I could castrate you ever morning for the rest of your natural life, which, really, we don't know how long it is. There is no bottom of suffering, John. I learned that a long time ago in Transylvania when I lost my best friend. You'll never have a best friend, John. Sometimes I feel bad about it but I don't bad about anything for long."

John struggled to stay upright. There was no reason to beyond thinking that if he went still, the bees would get even more violent. The scream would not come out, the apology The Colonel wanted but did not deserve would not come out. The Colonel's point did not elude him and the knowledge that he was beaten did not do so either. This was likely the last time he would ever resist anything he was ordered. Elsie Starlite was going to die and so were most of his other classmates. The Men in Black were likely already en route to see Rudy Kazanian.

"You're an ungrateful little shit, John. You have a gift and you squander it. You know how amazing your gift is, Queerbait? You'll be feeling good enough to go to school tomorrow. You should savor that, John. It's going to be a very big day."

The Colonel was not wrong.

\*\*\*

Derek awakened at 5:30 and checked his bag. Yup. Still loaded with guns and ammo. He'd packed it the night before but did not want the feeling of tension and euphoria to get in the way of efficiency and causing maximum damage. He went back onto reddit and Youtube. He saw the goodbyes and insults mingled together and that, in a way, he had friends and there would be more likeminded people out there when he was gone. He'd always wanted to inspire people instead of things he said and thought falling upon deaf ears. Yup. Still loaded with guns and ammo as he had packed the night before. He'd always wanted to inspire people instead of things he said and thought falling upon deaf ears.

He ate breakfast. Maybe it would have been better if he could have pancakes or something or go to the diner but there was no time for that and nobody would understand why he wanted to do something special. His mother wouldn't have understood him hugging her goodbye and neither would his father. He wouldn't miss them and they wouldn't miss him anyway. He ate cold cereal alone like he had so many mornings and took his five dollars for lunch like he had so many mornings. This was out of force of habit. It hadn't even occurred to him that he'd be dead after murdering several of his classmates before he got to spend it.

Derek got on the bus, putting on headphones and zoning out with his murder mix. He focused on the human mannequins walking down the hallway and how he was going to start popping heads. Cheerleader. Quarterback. Class president. Cliches but it didn't matter. That cunt Natalie. That whore Katelyn. That dumb slut Trina. Kyle. Kyle. Becky. Becky. Kyle. Becky. Splat. Think only of the bodies that are going to hit the floor because that's what you're doing today, that's what matters. He let the traces of humanity fade into an intercut of headless dummies in cheerleader uniforms splaying their legs open, exposing juicy, wet…no. Don't get a boner. That's not what this is about.

A moment later, he decided to let himself get this boner. It would be his last one and it's not like he had a girlfriend to use it on. He imagined the bodies without offending faces and how they were waiting for him and they secretly desired him, understanding that he had conquered them. And he was going to conquer them. He let it stir in him. This was going to be the best day of his life. He wouldn't have time to fuck those corpses, even if a part of him wanted to. But he could sure as hell imagine it, taking in the squishy delights of everyone he wanted. Ahhhh…finally none of these bitches could ever say no again. On other days, he tried to push these thoughts away but this was the last day of his life.

He was going to wait to the passing period before lunch to open fire because so many would be herded into the hallways and he could cut them off before they made it out. Shit. These first couple periods would be hell. The morning was a hundred Christmas Eves stacked one atop the other and resting upon his chest to make it hard to breathe. His eyes occasionally cut away to the visions of mannequin cheerleaders and their heads burst like cherries and the blood raining down in the hallways. He was dancing in that blood, light as air, free, finally free from the things that held him back, things like them.

He stared up Becky Chandler's skirt to try and take himself away from the pain of waiting. The visions might have made the world lighter and given phantom feet the wings to dance but he needed something else. Becky Chandler's thighs would be that thing. Kyle Pruitt was a lucky man plowing Becky Chandler. Maybe he could spare Becky Chandler in exchange for a blowjob. He could escape with Becky Chandler and he could survive and they could be boyfriend and girlfriend and fuck and suck and fuck and suck and fuck and…

NO! He wasn't going to stay alive through this. He wasn't going to sell out just because of that whore Becky Chandler. He wanted to grab the gun and finish her right now. Fucking bitch, distracting him with her legs and seducing him when he needed to keep his head in the game. He could have let this make him start prematurely. He couldn't let this make him start prematurely. Had to focus. Mannequins with burst heads. Pools of blood. Dead cheerleader cunt. Maps of the hallway that he'd trodden down again and again and again.

Another class and it was Becky Walden. Becky Walden's cleavage was worth his attention. She didn't jocks or anything. Becky Walden wasn't that stuck up but she was stuck up enough and none of them wanted him. None of them knew that he was coming for them and that he had all those guns and was going to paint the hallways with their blood. He could cut

Becky Walden the blowjob deal and she might take it though he'd heard she didn't really put out. He almost didn't want to kill Becky Walden. He might not kill Becky Walden. If she got in the way, he would kill her but he didn't need to kill her.

He got called upon to talk about The Old Man and the Sea. He didn't want to look like he was zoning out or staring at Becky's tits or had something else on his mind.

"It's an allegory about success. He wasn't going to catch that fish but he was noble for intending to catch it. It doesn't matter that the sharks took it away from him, he was still strong and determined and that's what counts."

"Very good, Derek," said Ms. Carswell. Maybe she wouldn't have to die. Maybe. He felt dizzy. There was a plan and he was going to stick with it. Wait for the lambs to herd themselves to the slaughter. No sentimentality. This isn't about who was good to you. This is about who is a part of this and who's gonna get it. Which is everyone possible. She was nice but it was her job to be nice. She was probably hot twenty years ago and when she was, she wouldn't have sucked your dick, so stop pretending you were attached.

Derek ended up in the bathroom crying. He was mad at himself for doing it. None of them had earned his tears or his compassion. It wasn't too late to stop this. It was too late to stop this. They'd called it down upon themselves through their hate and their neglect and their stupidity and their refusal to accept the world as it actually was. Still, he cried. Still, he dry heaved. He'd been working the last few days to prepare himself to be beyond this kind of bullshit. He wasn't beyond that bullshit. He was a human being who was about to kill a bunch of other human beings and his ability to pretend to be anything but was breaking down. He could tell someone and they could put him somewhere and he could get better and....

He regained his bearings. He wasn't the one who needed to get better. FUCK. This wasn't hard. This was what he needed more than anything, the thing he'd been working up to his whole life. That was probably why the jitters. Everybody gets nervous when they're about to do the most important thing they've ever done. Putting an end to these people was a higher calling and nothing could be that noble. He washed his face. He threw up again. He put his headphones back in and he went to his locker to gear up.

Hunting knife. Assault rifle. Glock. Second Glock. He wished he'd made some bombs or something that could clear a room faster. The assault rifle could do the job but a boom was so much more dramatic. Derek was not a science whiz. He was, however, smart enough to have two identical backpacks, one of which was full of books and got switched out before class so he wouldn't be rattling around all day with a bunch of guns. He grabbed his arsenal, pulled the assault rifle and lay in wait for everyone to come down this hall to stampede toward lunch, only to get peppered with bullets.

The next few moments felt impossibly slow. He had thought that time would start to trickle out and every second would feel like an infinity as he went about his hunt. These were, after all, the most important moments of his short, tempestuous and sad life. The next few moments felt like an eternity, stretched out into frustrated longing that could never possibly end. He first caught sight of that little faggot, John, who for some reason was not surprised to see him armored up. John was looking at something behind him, possibly as some kind of diversion .John looked shocked to see that but not to see a heavily armed Derek about to shoot him.

Derek was reaching for the trigger but something stopped him. A searing pain, a tear, a horrible warm, shredded feeling emanating from his stomach. His finger hesitated on the trigger, then his eyes wandered down to see just what had caused John's mouth to fly open. Blood, flesh, bits of gut were flying. It was a tiny hole but it felt miles wide and it felt like someone had taken a hot drillbit to it. It was a tiny hole but pieces of him were flying out of it. It had come from behind him and flown through. Some asshole had had the nerve to shoot him.

There was a fat man in his thirties in a skimask, black t shirt, cargo shorts. He was holding a pistol. Derek turned the assault rifle on him, trying to take aim but a second shot flew forward, catching him in the gut again. He staggered, the grip on the assault rifle loosening. A third shot followed and a lot more of Derek than he ever thought he would see flew out. Slower. Hotter. Sadder. Crueler. The gun dropped. Then Derek dropped. The last thing Derek saw before life mercilessly choked from his body was an excited John rushing over to the fat guy and giving him a gigantic hug. Derek died not understanding that this was the one time in his life that John had seen a good guy with a gun.

***

Mrs. Thackeray answered the door to find two familiar androgynous figures in blocky black suits outside. They had come to dinner a few times and seen each other at events but she did not know if behind the sunglasses they recognized her and registered her familiarity at all.

"Hello," said the block-breasted shorter one, "we are associates of your husband, the Colonel's. May we interest you in some photographs of your family?"

There was a weird fog in Mrs. Thackeray's head, a familiar buzzing noise and then a soft, film of joyfulness and warmth. She had thought there was something weird about these guys and seeing them at this time of day with that kind offer but she no longer thought it. She did not think about why she no longer thought about it. There was no reason for her to assume that anything like that had occurred. The weather was pleasant, she loved her husband, she loved her son and she really could use some nice photographs of her family.

"Ooh, yes! I'd love some. How much?"

"A dollar," said the tall one.

"Let me get my purse," said Mrs. Thackeray.

Mrs. Thackeray was not deceiving them to try and figure out what to do. Mrs. Thackeray had taken many blows to the head, endured years of marital rape and been exposed to so many things that made no damn sense at all that she had grown weird and complacent and developed many complicated defense mechanisms in her mind to combat suspicions that her life was anything beyond perfect. She smiled as she handed the tall MIB a dollar.

"Here you go! Thank you so much for thinking of me!"

"Oh, you are most welcome," she said as the MIB handed back a stack of Polaroids of John and The Colonel, several of

131

them very professional looking. She thumbed through them, a distant smile on her face and a song and a buzz playing in her poor, beleaguered head.

"Is your husband at home?" asked the small one.

"Would you like me to go get him?" she asked, "He is out in the garage."

"If it's not too much trouble, Miss," the tall one replied, "that sounds swell."

Colonel Thackeray was in the garage. He was naked. In one hand, he held his erect penis. In the other, he held a hammer with which he was killing squirrels. He had nailed them down to the table by their tails so that they could not wiggle away. There was nothing sporting about this setup and that's how The Colonel liked it. Smush. Snap. Crack. Splatter. Mrs. Thackeray quietly watched, not wanting to disturb her husband. She hoped he would take notice of her and inquire why she was out there and not NO her husband was a good man and he would never mistreat her, even for intruding on his special time.

It seemed now as if he was using his special time to get away from something. Maybe he needed a blowjob and a big stack of pancakes or a chicken fried steak. He looked at her, not angry and wildeyed as he usually would be but solemn and crestfallen.

"What? Do you need for something? Is Lafftrack busted?"

Mrs. Thackeray shook her head.

"No, dear, Lafftrack is fine. You fixed him. Things you fix stay fixed. There are two people from your work to see you."

The Colonel got his military uniform on and grabbed a sawed off shotgun. He took a long puff of his pipe and a long swig of something from a hip flask, then went to join the company. He looked in the vacant, glassy eyes of his wife, hoping to find fear in there. If there was still fear, he hadn't broken her over all these years. If she were in there, he would want her to hold him right now. She might have been more comfort than these squirrels whose skulls he was smashing. But she wasn't. There was only so much a person like her could take in and he had known that and he had flooded her mind with abuse and confusion and gaslighting until it could no longer object to him. This shell of a wife couldn't sympathize with him because it couldn't understand that he made mistakes. Because he couldn't understand that he made mistakes.

"Stay here," said The Colonel, kissing his wife, possibly goodbye. She'd been such a great piece of ass when she was younger. There might even have been a time when he felt something akin to love for her or the closest thing to love that he felt for anyone that wasn't Crenshaw.

"Yes, dear. Have fun with your friends."

"Oh, I will," said The Colonel, smiling through gritted teeth.

He entered the house through the garage, whispering to the voice within the walls.

"Lafftrack, power down."

The studio audience in the walls replied with an indignant "oooooh".

"Power down."

Lafftrack gave no indication of whether it was going to obey or disobey. He was not sure how loyal the voice in the walls was. It had been installed by the Agenda and was standard issue. The MIBs might have already hacked into it and the moment he padded his way to the door, there would be a loud applause or a howling laughter as loud as its volume controls could muster. On his best day, Colonel Thackeray trusted no one and The Colonel had a feeling that this was far from his best day. He was grateful to reach the door without a loud fanfare. When he swung it open, the MIBs on the other side certainly got one.

"Not today, you cocksuckers!" The Colonel shouted, knocking both of the MIBs on their asses with a shotgun blast. His Jeep was in sight and he hoped he could get to it before they rose up and tased him or trapped him in a forcefield or an alternate dimension.

His dash stopped cold though at the sound of whirling helicopter blades and cars driving up en masse. He was foolish to think that there would only be the two of them. Thackeray was a big fish and he'd given the Agenda the best years of his life. Six black limos and six or seven black helicopters were on the scene and they were loaded with MIBs or worse. Thackeray could try to shoot his way out of this and he'd kill a lot more people than anyone else would but he wouldn't kill enough before going down.

The MIB on the ground got up, leaking technoorganic plasm as it shouted to him.

"Colonel Thackeray, you need to relax. There is nothing wrong here. This is standard operating procedure and you are going to be fine. You could stand down now. It would be alright if you stood down now."

"Yes," said the other shotgunned MIB, "I agree. Standing down is the best thing you could do right now."

The shotgun dropped. The Colonel's hands went up. His eyes closed. He waited for the bullets. He waited for The Devil to finally meet up with him and make eternal sport of his deeply soiled soul. The Colonel waited for death but instead got the momentary sting of a stun dart, a swimming head and a descent into darkness and emptiness and chaos. He enjoyed the nothingness, rare moments of calm that were the opposite of everything he lived by. He was going to awaken to something completely unlike that.

"Shit," was the first thing the Colonel had to say when his eyes opened onto the set of the 70s gameshow Matchgame. He struggled to his feet, resting against the podium.

"Shit," said Count Dracula, "is an understatement, my dear Colonel. Welcome to Matchgame 2018. I am your host Count Dracula."

He looked out onto the panel. This was serious. The Gay Agenda did not unfreeze Charles Nelson Reilly for just anything. He should probably have just taken the Cyanide capsule. He bit down finding only his tongue. Thackeray spat blood on the floor and suppressed tears like he'd never suppressed tears in his life. The Lafftrack in the walls expressed cruel amusement as he did. He didn't let it get to him. He knew what Lafftracks were for.

"Settle down!" Dracula boomed, "We have a lot of ground to cover."

Lafftrack went silent.

"Now, let me introduce our panelists. First, liberal billionaire and reptile pawn, George Soros! How are you doing today, George?"

The silverhaired man waved to nobody in particular.

"Pretty good, it always pays to mastermind all dissent against a well intentioned right wing government."

Lafftrack shrieked out its approval. Nobody else did. Even Dracula was a little bit scared of Soros. Thackeray had met him a couple times at Bohemian Grove and knew that his wrath meant death or worse. Thackeray chucked politely. Maybe he could earn some points. Looking around the rest of the crowd, there was one guy he hoped was not who he thought he was.

"Next, the multiverse's greatest space prostitute, the queen of lust and longing, the Blue Beast, Kjennen Kas'sen!"

She looked gravely at Thackeray.

"I'm sorry, Colonel. I tried to help but everything is fucked up now. I'm sorry. I'm so sorry. The Grilled Cheese Consortium sends their best."

Lafftrack went into howling paroxysms. He could see in

her eyes that she meant it. He could also see in her eyes that she knew it was no consolation. Dracula did not give them time to exchange words. There was nothing else that could be said anyhow.

"Time and space traveler Professor Panda!"

A panda. He'd only heard rumors of what the world would be like under the panda empire. He'd also heard rumors that they were the ones who invented time travel for The Grilled Cheese Sandwich Consortium.

"Hi, Count. It's a pleasure to be here! Did you hear what happened when the panda bought fake Panda Chow?"

Dracula raised an eyebrow and smiled, baring fangs. This was hell. Whatever came after this was going to be awful and the spectacle made it infinitely clear.

"No, Professor what happened?"

"He got Bamboo-zled!"

Lafftrack split the room and shook it with the sound of its excitement. The Professor had hit maximum laugh potential. Thackeray did not know if he wanted to survive this ordeal after all. The bastards took his Cyanide capsule. Dracula gestured at the man who he hoped was not who he thought he was. Thackeray considered his luck and understood that it was almost certain the guy was. The tall, dark Spaniard in a slick silver suit had been on the lips of many dead men.

"Cannibal, assassin, jetsetting playboy and tango champion El Tiburon, fresh from murdering Colonel Thackeray's wife! How are you doing, El Tiburon?"

"Fantastic!" said the hitman, flashing filed teeth.

"It's very impressive work you did," said the Count. He turned toward nobody in particular.

"Do we have a clip?"

Lafftrack applauded. Thackeray steeled himself. Remembered the lessons he'd been taught about resisting torture. They were of very little help. He did not have information that he was concealing from them. He let a tear flow out as the film started on the wall behind the podia the panelists were seated at. El Tiburon was standing at the door. He knocked. Lafftrack laughed again. Thackeray knew he was just watching a film but still let out a "no, please!"

"Do you enjoy your work, Mr. Tiburon?" Dracula asked.

"Si, senor Dracula. And the Colonel's wife was very grateful. She hadn't been eaten out in years!"

Lafftrack slugged the Colonel clean in the heart. Behind El Tiburon, Mrs. Thackeray was opening up the door and gleefully chatting with one of the deadliest men in the world. She had spent a lot of time around one of the deadliest men in the world and had come out something like alive. The Colonel wished he hadn't beaten and lied and fucked the sense out of her and turned her into the sort of empty automaton that lets a suave killer in for a drink and seats him right in the livingroom. He had brought this upon himself and therefore brought it upon her. He kept focused on it, knowing there would be consequences to closing his eyes.

"And last," said Dracula, "but not least, Charles Nelson Reilly!"

The old, diminutive gay comedian in the giant glasses was literally a pallid reflection of his former self. His downcast eyes clad in the most flamboyant eyewear, were all business and all loss and all despair. None of these people was altogether human but at least most of them weren't dead.

"There was a time," said Reilly, "when this show used to be funny."

The old man looked around the room, sweat accumulating on his cold, white clammy brow. He got up and sang.

"But that was forty years ago, when we used to have a show!"

Lafftrack fell into yet another uproar. Mrs. Thackeray was on the livingroom floor, trying to wrestle El Tiburon off of her. He had a candlestick in his hand and dedication on his predatory and cruel face. She was struggling hard, finding bits of the things that he'd suppressed so she could be free of the brute on top of her. In the years before her conditioning, her gaslighting, her abuse, she would not have been a match for El Tiburon. She was even less of one in the film. The candlestick came down and she was out. He dragged her across the hall to the bedroom that they had shared, at least during the time since they had last resided in an identical house.

"Now," said Count Dracula, "let's play Matchgame. Panelists are you ready?"

"Ready for our closeup, Mr. Lugosi," Charles Nelson Reilly shouted back, "G'huh!"

The trademark laugh now chilled Thackeray's blood. Mrs. Thackeray was lying on the bed, El Tiburon was sharpening a knife. She was gagged but still the screams were escaping. She was right to do this because he was skinning her. Thackeray did not know how long he had been out or if this was happening before or after the gameshow they were on. The Gay Agenda had technology that made time and space meaningless. This could actually be broadcast live from right that second or the house could have been moved into the 79th century.

"Alright, here's the question :Colonel Thackeray's wife is dead because…what?" the panelists began to scribble on little posterboards on their podia, "Let me repeat, Colonel Thackeray's wife is dead because…"

Thackeray watches as El Tiburon began to flay his wife, tearing off giant strips of flesh. She was screaming, she was sopping red, she was begging and then she'd be in unbearable pain and a beatific smile would cross her face and then she would begin to cry and beg again. He was methodical as he tore the skin from her. He was eager, aroused and yet still consummately professional. He had never thought to do anything about people like this but admire them. He decided that it might be better not to die but to play their game and then kill that guy. Hmm. He hoped that Charles Nelson Reilly couldn't read minds like they said he could. Then again, this might not be something that was being done.

"It's real," said Charles Nelson Reilly in Thackeray's head, "you'd better believe it's real. You're not killing anyone today, though I do have to say this freak certainly deserves it."

"Thank you," he thought back at Charles Nelson Reilly.

"You shouldn't thank me yet. You need to answer. I hope you get some matches. I won't say you seem like a good guy because I know who you are but you don't deserve what we could do to you."

"Well?" Dracula asked Thackeray.

"Because I did not contain my child as directed to by The Gay Agenda."

Dracula nodded.

"A very good answer. Let's see what the panel has to say."

Kas'sen held up her posterboard.

"It's your lucky day," she said, "I put "because you failed to contain your child as directed by The Gay Agenda"."

Good. That was one. It was not his lucky day. Moreso not Mrs. Thackeray's. El Tiburon had left the room. She was tied to the bed, partially skinned crimson mess, trying to break free of her bonds. There was a sound in the distance, the first time the video had sound. Sizzling. Something was frying on a skillet. It shouldn't have been audible but it was loud. It wasn't hard to guess what it was.

"Looks like you've got one panelist, Colonel. Very good. I would not celebrate just yet, however. This game can take on many twists and turns."

Lafftrack let out a prolonged "oooooooohhhhhh".

"Now, onto our second panelist. Professor Panda…"

"Yeeeessss?"

El Tiburon returned, carrying a fried strip of meat. Thackeray could tell what it was. Mrs. Thackeray could tell what it was too. El Tiburon was dangling it over her face. She was shaking her bloodied, skinless head. In this distance was the sound of more sizzling, the sound of more of his wife cooking. She was screaming and he could hear it. Lafftrack was laughing louder, as if trying to cover it all up while simultaneously to make him hear that nobody had any sympathy for him or his wife. His wife who was being force fed a large chunk of her own fried flesh. Her eyes were open wide, tearful as she made sure to chew every bite several times.

"Do you have an answer for us, Professor Panda?"

"It's hard for pandas to decide on things, you know," he said.

"Why is that?"

"Because everything's always black and white for us."

Lafftrack ceased laughing and was beginning to weep openly. Its muffled sobbing was loud and offputting. Dracula clapped for the panda.

"Delightful! What a humorous little creature you are."

"HELP ME!" screamed Thackeray's wife.

Professor Panda held up the sign. It said "Rhubarb!"

Lafftrack switched back to laughter. The panel laughed. Dracula laughed.

Professor Panda held up his arms in a mock shrug.

"I put Rhubarb!"

"Well, this is getting very tense," said Dracula, walking back over to Thackeray, "you're going to need half the panel to get out of here without experiencing a fate worse than death."

"This show is already a fate worse than death!" shouted Charles Nelson Reilly.

Dracula nodded.

"A true comedy icon, ladies and gentlemen. I cannot say it enough."

Dracula approached El Tiburon.

El Tiburon held up only a drawing of an owl. Lafftrack let out wild applause. Dracula nodded solemnly.

"Well, it looks like we have two wrong answers and one match. Things do not look good for Colonel Thackeray. Not quite so bad as for his wife though."

El Tiburon had plunged his knife into Mrs. Thackeray's vagina and was vigorously fucking her with it. In, out, bloody mess, in, out, bloody mess, in, out, bloody mess. Mrs. Thackeray looked at the camera and The Colonel's eyes met hers because they had to. His too were full of tears. He'd known she was dead but he hadn't known just far they'd gone to make it feel awful. He let those tears fall, then braced himself for the final verdict from a 70s gameshow icon.

"I find myself concerned," said Charles Nelson Reilly to the host, "that the boy in question can find out how to get to Bohemian Grove. You know how to get to Bohemian Grove?"

"No," said Dracula, "how do you get to Bohemian Grove?"

"Practice."

Charles Nelson Reilly held up the sign that spared Colonel Thackeray a degree of torture that they couldn't even threaten him with for fear of ruining its impact. Thackeray breathed the air of a man granted breath anew. It read

"Because you failed to contain the child as directed by The Gay Agenda."

The Matchgame set revolved into the wall, leaving Thackeray and Dracula seated together in a colorless, featureless void. The vampire folded his clawed hands.

"This is a problem, Colonel Thackeray and you have brought it down upon yourself. What are we going to do about this? Call on Slenderman, Jeff the Killer?"

Thackeray shook his head, adrenaline surging through him, returning to his element.

"No, Count, there's another solution, a far better one than those clowns."

\*\*\*

When dawn came that day, Rudy Kazanian had slept an entire hour. The first thing he did was watch again as Derek gave his rant. He needed it close at hand, to know with his entire being exactly what he was heading out to stop. He pitied the kid more this time but again, not enough that he would not do what needed to be done. Derek had certainly shown that what Rudy committed to do needed to be done.

He ate breakfast at the I Hop because that's where he had several times decided that he would choose to eat if it came to pass that he had just one day to live. He ordered a stack of pancakes, a side of mozzarella sticks and coffee. He would need plenty of coffee. He considered telling Debbie the waitress that he had always had a crush on her but it wasn't like she'd know he was about to embark on a cool, secret suicide mission and therefore decide to fuck him. He also knew that the obit would be harder on everyone that felt they had some kind of connection. He ate his breakfast quietly, gratefully. Life wasn't total shit today. It might have been kinda nice to have more of it.

Rudy returned home and he kissed his mother on the cheek. Dad hadn't said goodbye. The last thing dad had said to her was probably something about the thermostat and how she needed to stop fucking with it all the time. Rudy's dad wouldn't have had sage advice or told his son he'd miss him. Rudy's mom deserved more than that. She had always looked out for him and always wanted the absolute best for her boy.

"Ma," said Rudy,"I want you to know that I love you and I appreciate everything you've done for me.

She raised an eyebrow. Though mothers are often accustomed to giving their sons everything, hearing praise was usually a warning sign that some shit was about to go down. She could smell it on him. He had been disappearing, sleeping weird hours and acting jumpy. It wasn't like her boy. Whatever it was had to be real bad.

"Rudolph, are you on drugs?"

"No, ma, I'm not on drugs."

"You could tell me," she said, "you could tell me if you were on drugs."

He didn't want to think about it.

"I know I could," he said. And he did know.

He hugged her.

"It's nothing. I just...I don't feel like I tell you enough that I appreciate what you've done. When.dad died, you were there for me. You're a good mother and you didn't deserve for him to leave you like that."

"He left us both, Rudolph. You didn't deserve it anymore than I did."

He chewed on this. She didn't deserve to lose a son like she might, like she lost a husband. And he never deserved to lose a father. She also didn't deserve a coward for a son. She had been fierce im defense of her child and such ferocity should not have been cut off at the source. He'd heard before that he didn't deserve it but he'd never quite felt that way.

"I love you, ma," said Rudy, "don't forget it."

Rudy's mother wouldn't forget it. She would never understand where he had gone or what he was doing this day. The fact that she didn't was a gift, it was as much a kindness as when the husband who wasn't cut out for life with a wife and kid took his life and set her free. Yes, she had known something was up with her son, yes, she held him a little bit tighter because there was something that told her that he was in trouble and something that told her she could do nothing about it but she could never grasp just what was going on.

Rudy Kazanian walked into a highschool wearing a skimask and carrying a pistol. Rudy walked down the hallways of said highschool without arousing any suspicion at all or being caught by an authority figure. Rudy bobbed, weaved, hit, waited, watched, got to know the route that Derek had drawn out and he did this without any visible consequences. He found this particularly disturbing, having recently checked out r/schoolshoot and found multiple assertions that your average highschool is not the metal detector fortress that the liberal media tries to tell you it is.

Removing these thoughts from his mind, Rudy observed the crowds until he saw the lunch rush was about to begin. Before John, he had not actually shot anyone. He hadn't entertained the thought of shooting anyone outside of power fantasies about defending hot ladies from Muslim rapists and being rewarded with big, sloppy blowjobs. He was not going to be rewarded for this. He was not going to be a hero. He was going to be a guy in a skimask shooting a child in broad daylight and hopefully running like hell and finding some place to lay low until the heat died down. He focused.

A skimask would have benefited Derek. Not posting about his exploits on Youtube and Reddit would have benefited Derek a lot. Wearing Kevlar would have benefited Derek a lot. Not choosing to shoot up his school would have really benefited Derek. There were any number of things Derek could do better but chief among those things would be watching his back. Derek should have watched his back.

Shooting someone who he knew could actually die was

harder on Rudy than shooting John. Knowing that several people had died because he failed to shoot the shooter dead would have been harder. He sent a bullet through that poor, sick, stupid kid. Then, when that poor, sick, stupid kid turned around, he fired another one and then another and then, from there, the little shit went right down. He felt a bit like vomiting, having not experienced the sight or smell of a mortal human taking on hot lead but he also felt compelled to do something else. After Derek's reign of terror got aborted in three quick shots, Rudy Kazanian hugged his only friend in the world.

Rudy had never thought there would be a context he would find himself in the happy embrace of the boy whose existence had up until recently offended him more than anything else in the world. And he had also never thought he would be literally jumping for joy at having caused the demise of a teenager. Rudy couldn't have had any idea what his life would look like. He had experienced several surprises. There was another in store.

"Attention students," said a voice over the PA, "this is Colonel Thackeray from the US Navy. There are two active shooters present in the school. But do not panic, the military has dispatched America's very own superhero. Delinquency Man is on the scene."

***

Derek was not the only one who needed to learn to watch his back. The tower of hate-forged brawn was right behind Rudy. It would have been good enough for it to just twist his head and break Rudy's neck. It did that right away, with a sickening snap, severing connection of body and brain and rendering the spine effective. He was going to slump to the floor and collapse into a heap of human cauliflower while the

145

one that killed him ran amuck in the school killing as it saw fit. It wasn't in the creature's nature to stop for the sake of decency, honor or propriety. It kept going.

As Rudy started to slide down the floor, The Delinquency Man delivered another punch, this one penetrating Rudy's anus, turning him into a human handpuppet, which was much more entertaining than the human cauliflower, not just a numb pile of dead organic matter but a humiliating, degraded, violated and wrecked toy. With a jolt, it held up the dead Rudy and pointed the corpse's face toward his. The voicebox crackled on.

"Look what you did, John. This man only wanted the truth in a complicated world. He only wanted to prove that you were out there ruining everything for everyone and he was right."

The Delinquency Man smashed the body on the floor shattering face and skull as it had his neck. It slid Rudy off its shitcovered fist, dropping him on the floor into a puddle of the contents of his own evacuated bowels. It improvised an awkward and excited dance in the puddle, splashing around like a happy child, spraying the excrement in all directions. John did all he could do; he grabbed Derek's guns, knife and backpack and sought out cover.

# HUNTING THE
# HUNTER

"I don't wanna be cliché or anything," Elsie Starlite would say to the press in a few days, "but he seemed like a nice, regular, boring kid."

She'd fight back sobbing because her mother and therapist reminded her that this boy did not deserve the tears that she had wasted on him. She was strong and she was angry and she was tired of thinking of him, so she would win.

"There wasn't too much that set him apart. I don't think he was super smart or really good at anything. I don't think he was slow. I think he had a crush on me, so I don't think he was gay. He just didn't fit in. Some people don't. They always say "I wish somebody would have opened up to him". Well, you know what? I did. And all those other people they say that about probably had at least one friend who did. The only reason anyone ever says it is so they can go back to blaming victims. It wasn't our fault. He was crazy. Maybe a few people called him names or shoved him into something but that's what being a teenager is like. It sucks."

There had been a tiny glimmer of platonic connection between John and Elsie. She had appreciated his candor and sympathized with his feeling out of place at the school. There was nothing else. If John had not been seen roaming the halls with a backpack full of weapons on the day of a massacre, supposedly having turned on his two partners, she would never have remembered John. Nobody would have remembered John. Nobody would have prayed, even as a simple test of their Christian mercy and compassion. Elsie would have forgotten John and John would have remembered

Elsie only in that vague, angry way people remember early unrequited crushes and assume that people who barely knew them were making value judgments and choosing not to like them instead of reacting to a stranger's immature obsession that lacked evidence or context. This was not even the worst thing she would say of John.

Everyone would have remembered John if he had gone down and played dead like he was supposed to. They would have remembered his smile. It's not that John smiled or had a prominent smile but when someone dies and nobody remembers them or has anything to say about them, the go-to piece of nostalgia that gets conjured up is that they brightened the world with their smile. Before school shootings, smiling wasn't half the deal it became in the same way that before dating shows nobody ever thought anyone didn't like music or would need to clarify that they did. Now that he was dodging around corners trying to avoid America's first superhero, there was no way anybody would remember John for his bright smile, or rather claim to remember John for his bright smile.

John was holding his breath. Hypothetically, Crisis Boys should have been able to hold it forever. He didn't know how acute the thing's hearing was, if it went by sense of smell, if they had augmented it with censors or even if it wasn't just a giant robot puppet piloted remotely by The Colonel. He hoped he would be able to make it out alive and escape to somewhere but he did not know where he would escape to. Was there anywhere he wouldn't be found? Was there anywhere they wouldn't just dispatch their monster again? Was there any way in hell he could get through the day without this creature getting to Elsie and tearing her limb from limb? He knew the answers to all of those questions was no. He had no plan before and had never been used to having a plan but now he incontrovertibly had no idea what to do.

However the Delinquency Man did hunt, it hunted a whole lot better than John hid. It had a habit of being right behind people, so much so that John tried not to turn around until he could immediately sense its looming presence and turn to face it. It had a habit of being behind people and it was finally right behind him. It also had a habit of sending people flying through doors. This time, it did so in a grandly superheroic fashion, uppercutting him straight through the door of a classroom. Splinters. Blood. Dizziness. Tables had been overturned for fire cover and students were crouched behind them. Though it was mostly concerned with him, he didn't want to risk the lives of all those present, those cowering from him and cheering for a monster that would likely kill several of them for fun when it was done with him. He made it to his feet and ran for the hallway.

It was there in the doorway, stomping towards him.

"Never fear, citizens! It is I, Delinquency Man, here to save you from this delinquent!"

Applause rang through the room.

"You go, Delinquency Man!"

"You the man, Delinquency Man!"

One girl even crawled out from under the table to flash him. John was mortified not because of the nudity but because The Delinquency Man might just interpret that as a form of delinquency and put its fist through her head. John exhaled. Let out a sigh and charged the monster, knowing that it was the only thing that would get it out of the classroom and back into the hallway. The students in that classroom would remember an American hero sauntering in. Then they'd remember the homicidal maniac shooter charging at The Delinquency Man, overextending his harm to throw an awkward and flimsy punch. Then they'd remember the clang of the shooter banging into a locker after being thrown several feet.

The back of John's head was bleeding. The hall was wobbling. It was sideways before he got his focus back and crawled off. John fought his way to his feet, stood up and pressed his back to a wall, keeping completely still. There was a gun in his hand and another couple in the backpack. He had one choice left and it wasn't what he'd been programmed for. He felt something almost like gratitude that The Colonel had dragged him to the firing range a couple of times. No son of The Colonel's was going through life without knowing how to handle a firearm.

He took off down the hallway. He'd need a place to hide if he was going to get the drop on it somehow. Where did people go to hide from the shooters? He'd seen this happen enough times and if people thought that there was an active shooter, they would gather in someplace big with a lot of cover. If there was a lot of cover, there was somewhere he could hide, hopefully without being ferreted out by the screams of anyone already hiding there. Maybe if he lied and threatened to shoot them, they would stay quiet.

He entered the library and looked around. It wasn't waiting to ambush him in there and he'd outpaced it enough that he could not hear, see or smell it. John was no tracker, no more than he was a soldier or really anything but a frightened fifteen year old whose military dad had put him through hell and a couple times taken him to shoot a gun. It wasn't in there. He was grateful until it occurred to him that wherever he went, it was going to follow and again, if it brought him down, it was not going to stop. Fuck. The people were hiding here from him and if he brought the thing he was chasing to them, it would all be for nothing.

She was there. She was hiding behind one of the tables alongside a bunch of others.

"Elsie!" John shouted, "You're okay!"

John did not think about the gun in his hand or that he

was in a fight with the world's first superhero and trying to kill him. For all the hate that presidential assassins and copkillers get, it would be a whole lot worse to be the first one to kill a superhero.

"Elsie, I'm doing this for you," he said.

"John, just put down the gun and everything will be okay," said Elsie.

John shook his head.

"Elsie, it's not what it looks like. You need to believe me, I'm doing this for you. I'm doing this to keep you safe."

"I don't know you, John," said Elsie, "you don't love me. I'm not impressed by this."

"Elsie, I love you, I'm trying to…"

"Could you just shoot me now?"

John had been shot, stabbed, immolated, blown up and stung by hundreds of bees. John had been exposed to every possible hurt his extremely sadistic and creative father could muster. What he had not been exposed to was being rejected by someone he loved or that he'd thought he loved. He felt potential shaking, twitching, dying. He felt a feeling like the gutshots he'd taken but there was no heat, only choking, only empty, only nausea, only wrongness. He felt like the only touch he'd ever know was the gun, the knife, the fist and the swarm of bees. He felt like Elsie Starlite was an emptyheaded pustulent cunt. He felt like Elsie Starlite controlled the sky and the tides and the weather and the ups and downs of his heart. He felt like Elsie Starlite was every beautiful he could ever have but never would.

It did not heal like the bullets or the knives. He did not think it ever would. He thought for a second that maybe he should have just done this job like every other job and taken Derek's bullets and gone about his life of getting killed again and again and again. It was surely nicer than this. He thought that for a second, then remembered he was not a horrible human being. Just a sad one and several lives were at stake. He didn't take his cover. He walked to the door, high on sadness and rage, high on "fuck this shit".

Red, white, blue and sheer disaster was waiting. He'd had the plan to hide behind something and start shooting and that plan wasn't going to happen. Plans were like that. Life was like that. Friends die. Girls turn you down. Parents treat you like shit for years. Homicidal superheroes try to tear you limb from limb for saving a whole bunch of lives. Life fucking sucked and maybe he didn't even die. He did something that someone who didn't know or care whether he could die would do. He slugged a superhero.

His fist hit muscle, his knuckles crackled, his bone snapped, his wrist lay limp and wobbly, bent backward into an impossible angle. He bit his tongue and let the limp wrist swing back and then forth, then back and then to the side and hit its face. With his other hand, he swung the butt of the rifle, taking The Delinquency Man by surprise but barely making it flinch. The Delinquency Man was unfazed enough that he could grab John by the top of the head and twist it backward. The spine and brain transmitted fuzz and John was not looking at things that were previously behind him but he wouldn't let himself fall.

He let his body fix his head and twisted it back into place with several horrible snaps. It worked. Somehow it worked. This body that had been fatally injured so many times was complying with his commands. He did the same with the wrist, the sound and the sight of it doing something he hadn't thought possible. He had surprised The Delinquency Man. And that meant time to shoot it in the gut two times before it could try and close again. John backed up, he fired, then he ran.

He rounded another corner and it gave him its back again. It was animal smart but not great on self preservation.

It had never dealt with something that could pose a threat. He went semiauto with the assault rifle and suddenly, there were holes. There was a miracle happening here and even in the sadness over Elsie and Rudy and everyone seeing him as a monster, he could appreciate the miracle. The monster bled. It turned around ready to strike him and he let it. He let it grab him and toss him into the lockers. He slumped down for a second, not appreciating the feel of metal slats against his back. But he got over it.

He got to his knees, shot it in the balls, and he rolled. As it let out its feral disapproval, he got to his feet and he hightailed it into another wing, the Delinquency Man not far behind. He was feeling more confident now. He was feeling like he could do this until he ran out of ammunition or until The Gay Agenda sent a limo full of MIBs to detain and force him to spend the rest of his life in one of those plexiglass cubes full of bees. It was better not to think about the plexiglass cube full of bees though.

The Delinquency Man's starspangled back was soon delivered once more to the one that it was hunting. It was stronger than it looked and it was faster than it looked but John was now dead sure that it was not smarter than it looked. The multitudes of teenagers that it had killed before the Colonel put on a cape on it had not usually been rocket scientists. He fired on it, letting several rounds of blazing, loud "Fuck this shit, I'm in pain" into it.

The rat-tat-tat, the plink, the splat. The recoil was rough and it threw him back some and he was still intimidated by that sound, that sound that had always meant pain and suffering. The weapon still felt wrong in his hand, still reminded him of being on the receiving end of those bullets. He had to trust it now, he had to walk the paths the maniacs walked and do as the maniacs did. It was hurting, it was dripping and it was enraged. It charged, smashing ribs, cutting and squashing organs, making him bleed internally. He headbutted it, felt the pain, felt the vertigo. His nose broke.

He shook off the numbness yet again. He headbutted yet again. He let the nose knit yet again, then broke the nose yet again. Fluid floated road and bonebit jangled in his brain but the dizzied, pained unkillable kid headbutted the moving mountain again and then again and then again. He struggled not to go down in the dark and let the light go out. It actually gave him space. The thing cocked its nearly impenetrable head in disbelief and backed away a moment. He used the space and he ran again. When he had some distance, he hit the floor.

He lay there on the floor and he waited. Hopefully, hitting it low would work. It was bigger than him, unstoppable from close range and no matter how much pain he could take, it would eventually dish out more. He hoped it would keep its back to him when it walked past and that there wasn't somebody watching through its eyes and feeding it information about him and where he lie in wait. It had stopped padding down the hall. It had begun to stomp. He had managed to get it upset and now that it was upset, it was vulnerable.

Finally, the plod of its snowshoe sized feet, finally the walking monolith, with its stench and trail of blood from the bulletholes in its back had come. It looked to its left, to its right, straight ahead. But it looked at eyelevel and it missed him. Life had not done John many favors but it handed him one this time. It approached and he lunged. He swung the knife at its heel and hoped for the best though never expecting it.

Threads of blood emerged from the cut, it stank like an open grave but it was bleeding again. John cut the other tendon. A beast like this didn't need armor. It could stand up to more punishment than any living being possibly could.

They should have armored it anyway and protected the heels. With another flick of the knife, John followed along the wound on the left leg, tracing along the dotted line of blood that he had made. And then he repeated the process. It trembled and howled, trying to turn but finding the tendons of its feet betraying it, feeling far too much pain to lift one foot and the other. John went to his knees, then point blank with the pistol shot the back of the ogre's knee point blank. He heard sinews snap, bones shatter as the bullet entered it. So he repeated the process with the other knee.

He pumped out another shot. Then another. It wheeled around, dizzy and in excruciating pain, it tried to remain upright but it could no longer support its gigantic bulk. He hadn't thought it possible. It was bleeding, it was yowling incoherently. Its back, peppered with holes from the assault rifle was exposed now, the costume shredded there. He got on top of the fallen colossus and with the knife, he followed along the trail of holes and tore and tore and tore and tore. It kept howling, it kept trying to get up but he had done a number on it. He had proven himself its equal in endurance and now he showed that he met it as an equal in brutality.

John disappeared from John's mind. There was now only stomping, shooting, reloading, stabbing, prodding. Just as it had been dogged and resolute in making sure its victims were completely pulped, so too was John at the same task. He did not know how long he had been at it, or whether his classmates had abandoned him and run from the school, called the police or FBI or Gay Agenda or what had happened. He knew only that he was breaking the monster's head open and making sure it could never stand up again.

The flesh beneath the mask had been greenish grey, covered in thick ingrown hairs and caked in dirt. It had once been dead perhaps and not stayed that way, so it was better for John to make sure that this time it would. He turned and threw up on the floor at the sight and the smell of the Delinquency Man's decimated head and the brain matter therein, then returned his focus to it to make sure it didn't get up. There was something among the chunks and the rot and the blood and the skull shards there, something shiny. It was a key to a bus station locker.

He picked it up. The school seemed to become hazy and out of focus as he lifted up the key. This time is was not just the result of too many blows to the head. This time it was something else entirely. He felt like he belonged to something and somewhere else now or like he always had. He walked out of the school and though he did not know where to find the bus station, he knew and it was close.

The bus station was full of skinny, pallid figures. Their eyes were surrounded by black circles as if stuck in a silent movie. They did not interact with each other and they did not interact with John. Most of them were just reading the newspaper, which featured no text but rather a series of cryptic symbols. John felt like there could be a time when he could read these papers but that time had not come yet. He avoided the figures, moving to a cluster of the lockers at the back of the room.

He approached the locker, 111B and put the key into the lock, opening it. There were three envelopes inside. Printed on each of them was a single word: choose. The envelopes were identical and John did not know if it was possible to choose right but only that he could choose but one. He did not know how he knew this anymore than he knew how he had been directed to the bus station or where it would lead. He examined each envelope but did not dare to touch any of them until he decided.

He reached for the middle envelope. He did not open it but the contents appeared in his hand. There was a little note, written in pink in a tiny, precise hand.

"You're getting there," it said.

There was also a bus ticket. There was no destination printed on it but he was certain that the station agent would take it. Though the station agent also seemed to be another holloweyed ghoul, there was no trepidation in John as he approached and handed it the ticket. It nodded and pointed to a bench for him to sit on. And so he sat.

He was not sure how long he'd sat there but it felt like forever. The black circled people got up and from benches and boarded their buses, none of them on the same one. There might have been a hundred of them catching various buses and taking their leave before his drove up, opening its doors to let him know the time had come. There was no fear or hesitation in John's heart as he got on.

The Greyhound was empty, the night long. John did not know where this bus was going or if he should have gotten on it. There was America out the window, cornfields, mountains, dusty, derelict factory towns. Smokestacks belching out decay. Abandoned circuses. Amusement parks that had not seen patronage in this century. Coyotes by the side of the road devouring something that may once have been a person. Figures in red robes chanting. Inhuman shapes burying a garbage bag full of something or possibly someone. Signs just reading "Perineum", "Pet Show", "Archelon Ranch?" and "Kittens for sale." There had been signs that made sense before but soon they were only these three signs.

The driver's face was smooth. It had no nose, no cheeks, no chin. It would occasionally let out a high pitched squeal and snort something from a tube. John could intuit that they were somehow alike but not how they were. He had no desire to ask how that was and knew that the driver could not answer and would not tell him where they were going. He knew where they were going but he did not. This way of knowing was new but it felt right. It felt like the way he

157

always should have known things.

After what might have been days or might have been minutes, the bus stopped. John did not need to thank the driver or to get off the bus. When the bus stopped, he was off the bus and standing in the shadow of a derelict monorail that ran above a seaside town. This town had been somewhere once, it had had potential and there were people that loved it. An unloved town does not have a saltwater taffy stand. An unloved town does not have a carousel. An unloved town does not have a skeeball arcade. There was no power at the skeeball arcade but he knew that there once was.

John walked the empty town and felt the seabreeze coming in. The sea was real, at least the sea was real. He'd been swimming a few times when he was very little. He'd been swimming the week before Sandy Hook, before he saw what guns and bullets did to people. The Colonel had never looked sad before that and did not look sad any time afterwards. He had thought at the time that The Colonel was proud that he was such a strong swimmer. The Colonel might have been proud but what he was proud of was the thing that John loved least about himself. John did not know what he loved most about himself.

Soon, he went from walking to running, dashing in the direction of the breeze. He was light and airy, he was fast. His body was no punching bag, no tin can to be shot at. He was made of flesh and blood and oxygen and not wounds upon wounds upon wounds. He was excited about something, he had had a happy memory. He had never suppressed it but simply placed a giant tarp upon it; he could still see it move and twitch and breathe underneath and know that there was something there and walk past it certain he had seen something move. Perhaps the beach would be the moment where he had last felt like a beloved son.

A man with long blonde hair and sunglasses wearing a

shirt with a crudely smiley face on it sat on a beach chair there, looking at an infinite grey green ocean. He seemed at peace. He seemed more than familiar.

"Are you Kurt Cobain?" John asked, "I love your music."

"I don't care."

"Wow, you are Kurt Cobain."

"Does it matter?"

John thought about it. John didn't like a lot of music but he did like this music and he did have the t shirt.

"I guess not," John lied, "do you like it here?"

"Does it matter if I like it here?"

John thought about it. He didn't know how he was going to get anywhere else and Cobain was the only company he had, if it was Kurt Cobain, which it most assuredly was, he'd have to get along with him.

"No."

The waves were calm. There were no seagulls, no fish, no boats. There was no horizon on the other end, only the possibility that there was sea and only sea and the Earth was only ocean or else life was waiting to crawl out from it and live and flourish and create. That would be nice. This town was beautiful and life would make it nicer. Life would make the whole Earth nicer. If the Agenda had already chosen to pull the plug, it wouldn't be that bad if life crawled out from this ocean and spread out from this town, making the world new again.

"I miss the saltwater taffy," said Cobain.

"I bet it was great."

"There was also a guy here who brought me a lot of smack."

"I'm sorry," said John.

They were silent again, watching waves lapping. John lost track of time as he did this, so was not sure if he'd sat and relaxed long enough before restarting the conversation.

"Who killed you? Was it Courtney?"

"Does it matter?"

John nodded.

"Who killed you?" Cobain retorted. There was nothing sarcastic or judgmental about it.

"Adam Lanza," said John.

"What else can I say?" said Cobain, though he was saying nothing. John finished the line in his head.

Cobain pointed out to the ocean. Something was rising, something huge and ominous, something whose scrutiny nobody could escape. John was surprised to see the owl rising from the water, cruel, wide blue eyes looking down on him, reminding him of the choices he had made at Bohemian Grove, choices that had cost Rudy Kazanian his life and had cost him the chance of ever being respected or remembered fondly by Elsie Starlite. He feared its eyes and what they knew but still, he jumped into the water and he swam for it.

The ocean had looked still but it was cold and it resisted him as he swam. He knew in the way that he knew the other things he had known since killing The Delinquency Man that he was welcome to swim back to the shore and Kurt Cobain and if he decided to swim back to the shore, then he would be right there. The owl was far and the shore was close and this was as thorough as his knowledge of either one's location went. He did not choose to go back to the shore.

Beneath the surface, children were reaching up, faces he'd seen at Sandy Hook, at the starting line of the Marathon. Their little hands brushed against him and sought to drag him under. They swam as fast as he did and were every bit as eager to see him drown as he was to swim to the owl. Hands, hands, hands, so many hands…he struggled against them, asking himself if they deserved to take him under. He had lived and they had died. Did his life truly have the weight of many others?

He struggled, even as he struggled with the question. He

swam on. He did not have any way of knowing whether it was or wasn't so, what he deserved and what he hadn't. He had watched Rudy die and Rudy didn't know what his life had been worth or how much could have been done with it. He felt selfish for watching Rudy die. He felt brave for facing The Delinquency Man, he felt brave for swimming this tide of grasping arms to reach the owl he had been so afraid of in the first place.

There was a plain white door in the owl's chest with a crystal doorknob on it. Though there were tiny hands upon his ankles pulling him down, John bobbed up to the surface. He reached for the door and turned the knob. The hands and the child bodies pushed and yanked harder on him, pulling him backwards away from it but he was determined and he had knees and elbows and a desperate and dire need to see just what was inside of that fucking door.

The room was white and empty, as if they were going to put a room in the room but never got around to it. There were no chairs, there was no table. There was nothing there to see except for something he was expecting, or rather had been told by this new intuitions that he should have been expecting. He was neither disappointed nor surprised to find The Beatnik from the party. The Beatnik had been referred to as The Devil and these could only have been The Devil's machinations. He was not happy to see him, nor was he angry to see him.

"For he's a jolly good fellow," the Beatnik sang, "and so say all of us, and so say all of us and so say all of us... champagne?"

The Beatnik extended a hand with a glass in it. John refused. The last time he'd had alcohol kind of went South.

"No thanks," John replied, "you're The Devil and you're responsible for my life being a series of tragedies one after the other."

161

"Well done, John," said the Beatnik, "it looks as if you have made it at last. I believe I owe you an explanation."

"To say the least," John snapped, "my only friend is dead."

"No," said The Beatnik shaking his head, "it's not like that at all."

John kept his guard up.

"Really? Because I saw Rudy die. That monster you brought to the school killed him. You guys have made my life hell."

The Beatnik laughed.

"Poor, simple John. Do you think the world so utterly devoid of nuance that a small cadre of people can make it like this? Rudy is not the one who is dead, you are?"

The voice of Kurt Cobain rang out in his head again.

"Who shot you?"

And he had replied "Adam Lanza."

"Yes," said The Beatnik, " you're beginning to understand."

John sighed.

"Beginning? I've been through so much already."

"You have, John. The worst of which is that you are dead and the world you currently see around you was created by your mother to deal with your death. This is your afterlife and her delusion."

The Beatnik continued the story:

"You came from Massachusetts originally and you lived by the sea. And you were pretty happy there, all things considered. You loved the water, you loved the people and you loved going to the boardwalks on the beach during the Summer. You'd swim and play games and eat ice cream and you were happy. You were such a happy kid and you were very well loved by your parents, the Thackerays. You were their third try for a son after two miscarriages. You were the one that survived, John. And to them, that made you the most special boy in the world.

Your mother got a job in Newtown, Connecticut and that meant you had to move. You were sad to be at a new school in a new place and you didn't like the kids in Newtown. Your mother felt guilty about moving you there, so when she reimagined everything, she saw your dad as a military man, someone who was strict and stern and commanding with his family and needed to move around a lot. It was hard for her to deal with the fact that she'd uprooted you all. Especially because of what happened at the school.

It's a lot for a mother to process, her son being shot by an animal like Adam Lanza. She wished she lived in a world where you had survived and that you could live forever. Every one of those parents wished for that and you were truly special to your mother. You knew her as a compliant idiot, a broken vegetable. Do you know why that is? Because that's how she felt when she lost you to Lanza. She felt ignorant and complicit in harm coming to you. She resented your father, so imagined him as an agent of abuse but also as a source of strength. She imagined him as the one who had given you the power to survive.

Why is the Colonel like this, you may wonder? It's simple. Your father did the worst thing he could possibly do in the wake of your passing: he abandoned her. Your death led to your father taking his own life. This is why your friend Rudy Kazanian's father committed suicide in this world that's become your afterlife. Rudy is the kind of person your mother believes would come about in the wake of a father's suicide. Your mother, by the way is half Armenian. Both Rudy and The Colonel are disgusting people, forged by the tragedy of your father's abandonment.

One of the vilest things about Rudy is that he denied all those tragedies that happened to you. He denied that a

163

person could survive them. Why is that? Why would your mother create a person who constantly questioned the validity of the narrative? Well, that aspect of Rudy is not your mother's doing but your own. The Rudy of this world has been rewritten due to your intervention. He was trying to get you to wake up and understand that this afterlife limbo you exist in is a crazed fantasy created by your mother. He is right, nobody should survive this.

Elsie Starlite represents the things you will never know because you will never grow up. You will never have a girlfriend or a wife because you died too young. Your attempts to save and get to close Elsie are your attempts to feel what it would be to know adulthood and your drive toward living. Elsie can't love you though because no matter how much you strive to emulate the living and keep this world together, it will never be able to have you in it as a healthy adult. This world's perfection cannot hold up.

And that, is where The Delinquency Man comes in. The Delinquency Man polices unsavory and adult behavior. It's the being that prevents people from indulging in baser impulses. It is all raging id, all anger at the state of a world where a young man can walk into an elementary school and start gunning down children. The Delinquency Man regulates morality and makes sure that nobody does drugs or has sex. He is represented as a tool of the system and is indeed powered by your mother's raging superego in a desperate attempt to create order.

Order in the world of your mother's raging grief and madness is chaos. All conspiracies converge. Invincible children are used as puppets to confuse and manipulate people. The Gay Agenda puppeteers the world for reasons nobody could possibly understand. Nothing is her fault because it's all the machinations of your father and shadowy cabals of space beings and religious freaks. And The Devil.

Your mother is big on the devil. She kept watching the world go to shit and kept trying to understand it but she always came up short. It took her son and it took her husband and that is all that really mattered."

John's head was in his hands. It made a lot of sense.

"So why are you telling me this?"

The Beatnik put a hand on John's shoulder.

"Because, John, you have earned this. Your afterlife has been a prison in a madwoman's memory and you deserve a chance to come out of it and rest in peace."

John liked the sound of resting in peace. He felt very tired lately and could now understand why. He had fought hard to get here and to defeat this mad narrative and at the same time, had fought for so long at its behest to preserve it. This life was not life and it now made sense to him why that was. Reality had felt flimsy and fragile and that was because it was. He couldn't die because he wasn't alive.

"How do I know I can trust you?" John asked. It was a fair enough question.

"I am known in this world as The Devil. The Devil is the unmaker, the ancient adversary. The Lord of Lies. In this case, the lies I represent are an opposition to the denial mechanisms that keep this reality intact. In reality, I am the truth and I am the light of reason."

"What do I need to do?" John asked.

The Beatnik indicated a door.

"Go through that door and as you do, embrace and accept death. And then you will be able to be at peace."

The door was grey and there were whispers behind it. He looked at it and he felt afraid. The world was telling him the truth now, so that fear could be the understanding that he was about to transcend all these evils. He had worked to live and now the thought that maybe he could rest had finally become scary.

"If you pass that door, you will give your mother closure. She will be free of this world in her imagination and you will be free of servitude to your mother's grief and insanity."

John thought about it. But not for very long.

"I don't think anything you've said is true. I've come to find out about The Gay Agenda and you're giving me the kind of insane conspiracy theories Rudy came up with. Show me The Gay Agenda."

The room faded.

\*\*\*

The world went pink and figures at giant podia were applauding John. A tall, pale, fanged gentleman in a cape sat beside a man in an immaculate suit, a reptilian, a Grey, an apparently albino man in sunglasses and a black turtleneck who may or may not have been The Beatnik wearing a different face and former president Barack Obama. Acolytes in rainbow robes were projected on various screens on the pink walls all around them, chanting like the redrobed ones he had seen before in languages he had heard before, some of them humming and keening, fervent and animalistic in their intensity. Looking around this room, John was now certain he was in the company of the Gay Agenda.

"The Devil lied to me. You guys were real. He was trying to make me walk through that door and die," John declared.

Balloons, confetti and tiny candies fell from the ceiling. A disco ball descended. A group of rollerskating monsters with fantastic abs skated in. A Frankenstein monster, a mummy, a werewolf and a gillman skated in and began to dance and skate furiously, indulging in complicated lifts, triple axels and impressive skate tricks as booming, repetitive, nightmarish music filled the room. John noticed that the tall, fancy man in the vampire cape looked like he really wanted to go down there and skate but for some reason wasn't going to.

"Welcome," said the pale, fancy man, "to Count Dracula's Spooky Roller Disco, the headquarters of the Gay Agenda!"

"This is not a spooky roller disco. I don't understand why you're trying to confuse me," said John.

The monsters, crestfallen, skated off. The acolytes on the screens heaved heavy sighs.

"Tell me," asked the albino in the big sunglasses, "did you like that?"

"No," said John, "it was completely pointless and a waste of everyone's time."

"Solid," said the albino, "real gone."

The rainbow acolytes vanished from the projected screens on the walls, replaced by a fat, middle aged bald man wearing a prominent police bag. He was being interviewed by a reporter. He was standing outside of the Thackeray home.

"So, tell us, what did you find in there?"

"Well," said the man with a badge, "I'd like to warn more sensitive to cover their ears or look away. This is some pretty grisly stuff."

The reporter looked at the camera.

"Well, you heard the detective's warning here, folks. Viewers with more delicate sensibilities should look away or cover their ears, what follows might be shocking."

The detective began to break down in tears.

"I'm sorry, I need a second."

"Sure, take your time."

This was another trick, John told himself. The new way of knowing told him that it was not. The new way of knowing told him that what was on the screen was intimately related to how he got there and to what was going to happen next. He braced himself, now aware that they were showing him something terrible and that he could not run from the knowledge there.

"The crimes began here. The shooter knocked his mother out. He flayed her alive, frying strips of her skin on the oven. He fed her her own flesh, then stabbed her several times."

The reporter fell to her knees, breaking down into choking sobs.

"How? How can that be? How could a person do that?"

The detective did something you'd never see on a news report. He hugged the reporter. They stood in their embrace, trying to understand how John's hypothetical depravity was at all possible. John's eyes widened. His knees trembled. Mrs. Thackeray had not been a great mother. Or maybe she had and he had no way of knowing. Mrs. Thackeray didn't deserve any more than Rudy had and now she too had been claimed by this conspiracy.

"I can't go on," said the detective.

"We can cut the tape," sobbed the reporter.

"I must go on," said the detective.

The tape cut out. There was only static. The robe acolytes blipped in and out before the face of Elsie Starlite appeared on the tv.

"He said he was doing this for me. Can you imagine? Why would I want him to do that? I had never thought he was capable of anything like that. I don't know if I'll ever sleep well again. He killed students. He killed his mother. He killed an American hero and his twisted mind, he did it all for me."

He had known in the library that she would never want him or want to be close to him. Hearing her say this was not surprising. This reminded him of the punches he'd taken and the bullets, all the times he'd been wounded so severely he couldn't feel it anymore. The Gay Agenda didn't have anything more to take. Whatever they were trying to do to him from here, it wasn't working well. Rudy and Mrs. Thackeray were both dead now and he was the one who was blamed for the whole thing. They had gone far to show the result of noncompliance. They didn't need to go any further. His brain and heart shut off as the screen showed Elton John playing a tribute song for The Delinquency Man.

The screens shut off. The Lafftrack from the walls grew loud, caterwauling its amusement. The tribute to the monster who he had sacrificed his future to kill should have made him feel ill but couldn't have been compared to the other experiences he'd had on this day and the loss of the woman he'd known as a mother. Still, Lafftrack had always gotten to him, had been a constant companion through the miseries and tortures he'd endured at home. He hated the sound of the braying machine. It couldn't have been laughing about anything good.

He was numb to the sight of Colonel Thackeray rising from the floor bound to a chair. The laughter got to him worse than that. The laughter got to him worse than the sight of the cloaked stranger from the gallery above swooping down and opening a fanged mouth, lowering it onto the Colonel's throat and tearing it out.

"I am Dracula and we are even now." Dracula's cold, feral eyes locked with John's.

"What do you mean?"

"You came here, so you are entitled to this reward. We have rid the world of the one who hurt you worst."

Lafftrack boomed with applause.

John rolled his eyes.

"What do you mean? He did all of this for you. This is your fault, not mine, not his, yours. And I don't get it. How is this The Gay Agenda? How do gay people benefit from you letting trans Muslims kill people with scimitars or tricking a couple of people into believing that Sandy Hook didn't happen. What do gay people gain from liberals hating guns?"

"Benefit?" said the Grey, "What is benefit?"

Dracula, Obama, George Soros, Andy Warhol and the reptilian laughed. Lafftrack echoed it and amplified it.

"Why do you think we would want to benefit gay people? We have far too much power to do anything even slightly beneficial to the oppressed."

John had not thought he understood the situation but now he understood less than he had before he'd gotten there. This made less than no sense now.

"If you don't benefit gay people, then how are you The Gay Agenda?"

Again, howling peels of laughter. Again, the conspirators were incredulous. What seemed common sense to them was utterly foreign to John. He hadn't had much life experience that did not involve getting shot at but he still felt that a person with a multitude of experiences would not have been able to divine what it was that they were doing and why they had chosen to do it.

"My boy," said George Soros, "The Gay Agenda is not called The Gay Agenda because it is gay. It is called The Gay Agenda because it is easy to blame gay people for basically anything. It was a good name. When people weren't sufficiently uncomfortable about having someone with what they thought to be irregular genitals in the bathroom, we told them that the Gay Agenda meant putting men in dresses in bathrooms to rape little girls. We did nothing even though we knew a man with guns was going to open fire in a gay club. And then we let gunlovers think that because of this, The Gay Agenda was going to take their guns. We sat back and watched transgender Muslim terrorists that we could have easily stopped go into Bowling Green, then suppressed the news and let them think that The Gay Agenda let the suffering of good, hardworking Americans at the hands of transgender Muslim terrorists happen because The Gay Agenda supported white genocide or something."

"But why? Who does this help? How do you guys gain from this? "

The conspirators looked back and forth at each other. John could see that they were very confused.

"Agendas are not people," the Count snarled, "Agendas are the opposite of people. Agenda is from the Latin for "to be done". It is simply to be done. We don't know where agendas come from and when they benefit us, it is almost entirely a coincidence. An Agenda is just done because it is done."

John pounded on the pink wall.

"You killed my friend and my family, you raised me to die for no reason. You don't protect anyone, you don't make anyone's lives better, you just hurt people for no fucking reason at all. You're monsters."

"We didn't say it was for no fucking reason. We just said we don't know why. And we don't. The Agenda does what it needs to do. You should be grateful."

"Why?"

"Because you made it here," said Dracula, "and that means we can give you whatever your heart desires and that you are now   qualified to replace your father as an agent of The Gay Agenda."

"Why would I do that?"

"Why does anyone do anything?" Warhol asked.

"I don't want to be like you."

"What are you going to do?" asked Soros derisively, "Help people?"

John shrugged.

"I don't know. What I want is a fake ID and a dufflebag full of money and to never see any of freaks again.'"

The Frankenstein monster skated back in with the dufflebag and handed it to John.

Again, things were not the same. The room filled with

light. John's body filled with pain, the accumulated pain of every time he was shot, stabbed, punched, beaten and stung. He let out a scream that made the world itself shake, that made all possible worlds shake. In all possible worlds, for a fragment of a second, all beings remembered mortality and remembered that life was a thing of value. They would forget this the first time they saw they couldn't buy their kid a new iphone. They would forget this the next time there was something shinier or tastier to buy or eat or fuck but for a sublime moment, all beings understood that decay and time were their masters and that love is all we have.

And all things went blank.

# THE INTERNET MADE
# ME DO THIS

"Let's not talk about men," said Colonel Bechdel, as she was tired of talking about men.

"Agreed," said Jon Benet Ramsey, "there are more important things in life."

"Was it worth it?" asked the Colonel, "What we put you through?"

Jon Benet sipped her chocolate malt.

"Measures like that are worthless."

"What do you mean?"

"Asking if pain is worth it."

Colonel Bechdel thought about the gruesome death of the woman across from her and all it had done to unite the nation in favor of something or other. They knew better. They always knew better. It was best not to question the Agenda. Agendas are bigger than all of us and encompass us even if they do not seem to be in our best interest. There was a buzzing in her ear that led her back from going astray into the realm of whys and wherefores.

"So, could you unpack that?"

"When you're a Crisis Girl, you spend a lot of time thinking about whether the world actually benefitted from your murder or whether it made you stronger or better. And whether you wish it didn't happen. You're taught by your handler that it's best not to think like that because it can't not happen and it's the nature of Crisis Girls."

"I'm sorry."

"You don't have to be. I was confused and upset when they brought me to you and I was in that bodybag and gasping

173

and trying to claw my way out. I hated you. I wanted to see my family again, even if they had done what they did, which they did."

"Yes."

"And you let them."

Colonel Bechdel shrugged.

"It could have been one of those fixed points in time."

"Do those exist?"

"Nobody knows or cares."

"So there you go. There are awards for going through the most shit, surviving the most killings, being the most oppressed but you know what's better than those awards?"

"What?"

"Not being murdered."

"Yeah," said The Colonel, eyes darting around the reststop Shirley Temple's.

"In comparison to being murdered, not being murdered is the greatest of all possible outcomes. Everyone wants not to be murdered."

"Yeah," said The Colonel, eyes darting around the reststop Shirley Temple's.

"So in the end, when we look at the pain we've suffered, it doesn't matter if it was worth it or not. It's still pain. It still hurts. There's no winners, no losers, just a bunch of people being hurt."

"Yeah," said The Colonel, eyes darting around the reststop Shirley Temple's.

"I'm alive and nobody's murdering me anymore. It's better. Or at least it's different."

"Yeah," said The Colonel, eyes darting around the reststop Shirley Temple.

# AND IN
# THE END

The face he looked into was luminous and bright and saintly. It was Mrs. Thackeray, the best possible Mrs. Thackeray, in the best moment of her life. She had gossamer wings, peppered with bullet holes, a diaphanous satin dress, covered in holes and blood and was holding an AK-47. This was surely another trick of the Agenda because the only person she could be was someone who simply did not exist. John, still wracked in pain, forced his mouth open to ask a question he didn't want the answer to.

"Are you The Bullet Fairy?"

"I am that which you say I am," said The Bullet Fairy.

"Thank you for the money," said John.

"It's not enough," said The Bullet Fairy, helping John to his feet. John looked around him. Fuck. He didn't want to be where he was. He knew he was walking in this hallway. He knew that not far from him, the Motherfucking Devil, Adam Lanza was waiting for him. He was a child there. And yet he was not a child and was here with a dufflebag full of money and The Bullet Fairy. She took his hand and led him around the corner.

"Do I have to watch?"

The Bullet Fairy nodded.

"Okay," said John.

He rounded the corner to find the child, whose eyes were wide at the sight of Adam Lanza. The boy stood, doe in headlights, knowing somehow what was coming and seeing that it was. The bullets flew and the child, John went down. The boy's eyes were closed but this time, he wasn't faking it. This time, the boy was dead.

"He's dead," said John to The Bullet Fairy, "I'm dead."

"You are. But you're not."

"How?"

"Through God," said The Bullet Fairy, "all things are possible."

"God?" John asked, about ready to launch into a tirade on behalf of the dead child on the floor at Sandy Hook.

"Thou art that," said The Bullet Fairy, "this is not the worst of all possible worlds."

"What am I supposed to do with that?" John asked.

"The best you can."

And then John returned to the world. It wasn't the best or worst one, it simply was.

**Garrett Cook** has a transgender girlfriend, several weird and horrific books to his name and very few fucks left. He is dying faster than you are.

# deadite press

**"WZMB" Andre Duza** - It's the end of the world, but we're not going off the air! Martin Stone was a popular shock jock radio host before the zombie apocalypse. Then for six months the dead destroyed society. Humanity is now slowly rebuilding and Martin Stone is back to doing what he does best-taking to the airwaves. Host of the only radio show in this new world, he helps organize other survivors. But zombies aren't the only threat. There are others that thought humanity needed to end.

**"Tribesmen" Adam Cesare** - Thirty years ago, cynical sleazeball director Tito Bronze took a tiny cast and crew to a desolate island. His goal: to exploit the local tribes, spray some guts around, cash in on the gore-spattered 80s Italian cannibal craze. But the pissed-off spirits of the island had other ideas. And before long, guts were squirting behind the scenes, as well. While the camera kept rolling...

**"Reincarnage" Ryan Harding and Jason Taverner** - In the 80's a supernatural killer known as Agent Orange terrorized the United States. No matter how many times he was killed, he kept coming back to spread death and mayhem. With no other choice, the government walled off the small town, woods, and lake that Agent Orange used as his hunting ground. This seemed to contain the killer and his killing sprees ended. Or so the populace thought...

**"Suffer the Flesh" Monica J. O'Rourke** - Zoey always wished she was thinner. One day she meets a strange woman who informs her of an ultimate weight-loss program, and Zoey is quickly abducted off the streets of Manhattan and forced into this program. Zoey's enrolling whether she wants to or not. Held hostage with many other women, Zoey is forced into degrading acts of perversion for the amusement of her captors. ...

**"Answers of Silence" Geoff Cooper** - Deadite Press is proud to present the extremely sought after horror stories of Geoff Cooper. Collecting fifteen tales of the weird, the horrific, and the strange. Fans of Brian Keene, Jack Ketchum, and Bryan Smith won't want to miss this collection from one of the unsung masters of modern horror. You won't forget your visit to Geoff Cooper's dark and deranged world.

**"Boot Boys of the Wolf Reich" David Agranoff** - PIt is the summer of 1989 and they spend their days hanging out and having fun, and their nights fighting the local neo-Nazi gangs. Driven back and badly beaten, the local Nazi contingent finds the strangest of allies - The last survivor of a cult of Nazi werewolf assassins. An army of neo-Nazi werewolves are just what he needs. But first, they have some payback for all those meddling Anti-racist SHARPs...

**"White Trash Gothic" Edward Lee** - Luntville is not just some bumfuck town in the sticks. It is a place where the locals make extra cash by filming necro porn, a place where vigilantes practice a horrifying form of justice they call dead-dickin', a place haunted by the ghosts of serial killers, occult demons, and a monster called the Bighead. And as the writer attempts to make sense of the town and his connection to it, he will be challenged in ways that test the very limit of his sanity.

**"Whargoul" Dave Brockie** - It is a beast born in bullets and shrapnel, feeding off of pain, misery, and hard drugs. Cursed to wander the Earth without the hope of death, it is reborn again and again to spread the gospel of hate, abuse, and genocide. But what if it's not the only monster out there? What if there's something worse? From Dave Brockie, the twisted genius behind GWAR, comes a novel about the darkest days of the twentieth century.

## AVAILABLE FROM AMAZON.COM

**"Brain Cheese Buffet" Edward Lee** - collecting nine of Lee's most sought after tales of violence and body fluids. Featuring the Stoker nominated "Mr. Torso," the legendary gross-out piece "The Dritiphilist," the notorious "The McCrath Model SS40-C, Series S," and six more stories to test your gag reflex.
*"Edward Lee's writing is fast and mean as a chain saw revved to full-tilt boogie."*
- Jack Ketchum

**"Ghoul" Brian Keene** - There is something in the local cemetery that comes out at night. Something that is unearthing corpses and killing people. It's the summer of 1984 and Timmy and his friends are looking forward to no school, comic books, and adventure. But instead they will be fighting for their lives. The ghoul has smelled their blood and it is after them. But that's not the only monster they will face this summer . . . From award-winning horror master Brian Keene comes a novel of monsters, murder, and the loss of innocence.

**"The Dark Ones" Bryan Smith** - They are The Dark Ones. The name began as a self-deprecating joke, but it stuck and now it's a source of pride. They're the one who don't fit in. The misfits who drink and smoke too much and stay out all hours of the night. Everyone knows they're trouble. On the outskirts of Ransom, TN is an abandoned, boarded-up house. Something evil happened there long ago. The evil has been contained there ever since, locked down tight in the basement—until the night The Dark Ones set it free . . .

**"His Pain" Wrath James White** - Life is pain . . . . . . or at least it is for Jason. Born with a rare central nervous disorder, every sensation is pain. Every sound, scent, texture, flavor, even every breath, brings nothing but mind-numbing pain. Until the arrival of Yogi Arjunda of the Temple of Physical Enlightenment. He claims to be able to help Jason, to be able to give him a life of more than agony. But the treatment leaves Jason changed and he wants to share what he learned. He wants to share his pain . . . A novella of pain, pleasure, and transcendental splatter.

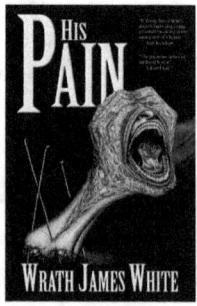

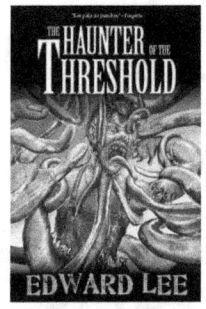

**"The Haunter of the Threshold" Edward Lee -** There is something very wrong with this backwater town. Suicide notes, magic gems, and haunted cabins await her. Plus the woods are filled with monsters, both human and otherworldly. And then there are the horrible tentacles . . . Soon Hazel is thrown into a battle for her life that will test her sanity and sex drive. The sequel to H.P. Lovecraft's The Haunter of the Dark is Edward Lee's most pornographic novel to date!

**"Baby's First Book of Seriously Fucked-Up Shit" Robert Devereaux -** From an orgy between God, Satan, Adam and Eve to beauty pageants for fetuses. From a giant human-absorbing tongue to a place where God is in the eyes of the psychopathic. This is a party at the furthest limits of human decency and cruelty. Robert Devereaux is your host but watch out, he's spiked the punch with drugs, sex, and dismemberment. Deadite Press is proud to present nine stories of the strange, the gross, and the just plain fucked up.

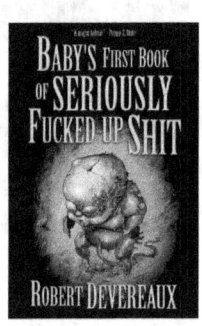

**"Highways to Hell" Bryan Smith -** The road to hell is paved with angels and demons. Brain worms and dead prostitutes. Serial killers and frustrated writers. Zombies and Rock 'n Roll. And once you start down this path, there is no going back. Collecting thirteen tales of shock and terror from Bryan Smith, Highways to Hell is a non-stop road-trip of cruelty, pain, and death. Grab a seat, Smith has such sights to show you.

**"Apeshit" Carlton Mellick III -** Friday the 13th meets Visitor Q. Six hipster teens go to a cabin in the woods inhabited by a deformed killer. An incredibly fucked-up parody of B-horror movies with a bizarro slant

*"The new gold standard in unstoppable fetus-fucking kill-freakomania . . . Genuine all-meat hardcore horror meets unadulterated Bizarro brainwarp strangeness. The results are beyond jaw-dropping, and fill me with pure, unforgivable joy."* - John Skipp

## AVAILABLE FROM AMAZON.COM

# deadite press

**"Earthworm Gods" Brian Keene -** One day, it starts raining-and never stops. Global super-storms decimate the planet, eradicating most of mankind. Pockets of survivors gather on mountaintops, watching as the waters climb higher and higher. But as the tides rise, something else is rising, too. Now, in the midst of an ecological nightmare, the remnants of humanity face a new menace, in a battle that stretches from the rooftops of submerged cities to the mountaintop islands jutting from the sea. The old gods are dead. Now is the time of the Earthworm Gods...

**"The Complex" Brian Keene -** There was no warning. No chance to escape. They came suddenly. Naked. Bloodthirsty. Sadistic. They descended upon the Pine Village Apartment Complex, relentlessly torturing and killing anyone they could find. Fearing for their lives, the residents of the complex must band together. Eleven strangers. The only thing they have in common is the unstoppable horde that wants to kill them. If they are to make it through the night, they must fight back.

**"An Occurrence in Crazy Bear Valley" Brian Keene-** The Old West has never been weirder or wilder than it has in the hands of master horror writer Brian Keene. Morgan and his gang are on the run--from their pasts and from the posse riding hot on their heels, intent on seeing them hang. But when they take refuge in Crazy Bear Valley, their flight becomes a siege as they find themselves battling a legendary race of monstrous, bloodthirsty beings. Now, Morgan and his gang aren't worried about hanging. They just want to live to see the dawn.

**"Entombed II" Brian Keene-** It has been several months since the disease known as Hamelin's Revenge decimated the world. Civilization has collapsed and the dead far outnumber the living. The survivors seek refuge from the roaming zombie hordes, but one-by-one, those shelters are falling. Twenty-five survivors barricade themselves inside a former military bunker buried deep beneath a luxury hotel. They are safe from the zombies...but are they safe from one another?

**"A God of Hungry Walls" Garrett Cook -** When you are within my walls, I am God. I have always been here and I will always be. I have complete dominion. I control what you see, what you feel, and how you think. I will bend reality to whatever I wish. I will show you your worst fears and make you indulge in your darkest desires. Your pain is my pleasure. Your tears are my ambrosia. Your despair is my joy. I will break you. I will ruin you. Once you enter me, there is no escape. I will own you, forever.

**"The Lucky Ones Died First" Jack Bantry -** Crushed heads, entrails, and piles of body parts are littering the woods surrounding the quaint English vacation town of Hambleton. A hungry cryptid is on the loose and is biting and tearing to pieces whoever and whatever it can catch. Now the residents must team up with a former-Nazi Bigfoot hunter to save themselves and their livelihood from this monstrous horror. People must fight. Many of them will not live to see the next day…

**"Clickers" J. F. Gonzalez and Mark Williams-** They are the Clickers, giant venomous blood-thirsty crabs from the depths of the sea. The only warning to their rampage of dismemberment and death is the terrible clicking of their claws. But these monsters aren't merely here to ravage and pillage. They are being driven onto land by fear. Something is hunting the Clickers. Something ancient and without mercy. *Clickers* is J. F. Gonzalez and Mark Williams' gore-soaked cult classic tribute to the giant monster B-movies of yesteryear.

**"Spermjackers from Hell" Christine Morgan -** Let's summon a succubus, they said. It'll be fun, they said…We were wrong. Really fucking wrong.The demon is not what we thought and it's making horrible things happen. People are cutting into each other's junk, some guy is fucking his dog, and sex slugs from Hell are raping us and stealing our semen in order to build a goddamn hive! We didn't mean for any of this. But we're gonna fix it… Just after a few more beers and bong hits.

## AVAILABLE FROM AMAZON.COM

# deadite press

**"Header" Edward Lee** - In the dark backwoods, where law enforcement doesn't dare tread, there exists a special type of revenge. Something so awful that it is only whispered about. Something so terrible that few believe it is real. Stewart Cummings is a government agent whose life is going to Hell. His wife is ill and to pay for her medication he turns to bootlegging. But things will get much worse when bodies begin showing up in his sleepy small town. Victims of an act known only as "a Header."

**"Punk Rock Ghost Story" David Agranoff** - In the summer of 1982, legendary Indianapolis hardcore band, The Fuckers, became the victim of a mysterious tragedy. They returned home without their vocalist and the band disappeared. A single record sought by collectors, a band nearly forgotten, and an urban legend passed from punk to punk. What happened to The Fuckers on that tour? Why was their singer never seen again? No one has been able to say. Until now…

**"Zombies and Shit" Carlton Mellick III** - Twenty people wake to find themselves in a boarded-up building in the middle of the zombie wasteland. They soon discover they have been chosen as contestants on a popular reality show called Zombie Survival. Each contestant is given a backpack of supplies and a unique weapon. Their goal: be the first to make it through the zombie-plagued city to the pick-up zone alive. But because there's only one seat available on the helicopter, the contestants not only have to fight against the hordes of the living dead, they must also fight each other.

**"The Book of a Thousand Sins" Wrath James White** - Welcome to a world of Zombie nymphomaniacs, psychopathic deities, voodoo surgery, and murderous priests. Where mutilation sex clubs are in vogue and torture machines are sex toys. No one makes it out alive – not even God himself.

*"If Wrath James White doesn't make you cringe, you must be riding in the wrong end of a hearse."*
-Jack Ketchum

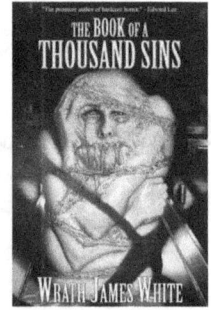